THE POISONED PEN

The Paisley Sterling Mysteries

Cemetery Silk
The Plague Doctor
The Paper Detective
The Cradle Robber
The Poisoned Pen
The Sow's Ear

Published by Wildside Press

THE POISONED PEN

The Fifth Paisley Sterling Mystery

by

E. JOAN SIMS

The Borgo Press
An Imprint of Wildside Press

MMVII

Copyright © 2007 by E. Joan Sims

All rights reserved.
No part of this book may be reproduced in any form without the expressed written consent of the author and publisher. Printed in the United States of America

FIRST EDITION

CONTENTS

Chapter One 7
Chapter Two 13
Chapter Three 17
Chapter Four 22
Chapter Five 27
Chapter Six 32
Chapter Seven 38
Chapter Eight 44
Chapter Nine 51
Chapter Ten 56
Chapter Eleven 61
Chapter Twelve 66
Chapter Thirteen 75
Chapter Fourteen 81
Chapter Fifteen 86
Chapter Sixteen 94
Chapter Seventeen 103
Chapter Eighteen 110
Chapter Nineteen 116
Chapter Twenty 122
Chapter Twenty-One 128
Chapter Twenty-Two 134
Chapter Twenty-Three 140
Chapter Twenty-Four 146
Chapter Twenty-Five 152
Chapter Twenty-Six 157
Chapter Twenty-Seven 162

About the Author 167

DEDICATION

To my grandparents,

Ada Atherton Mohon and Hyla Mohon

For all the wonderful memories

CHAPTER ONE

I liked to think of myself as a product of the New South: an energetic, intelligent woman who has taken advantage of every opportunity to achieve a fairly comfortable degree of financial and personal freedom by her middle years—early middle years, that is. But surrounded, as I was, by graceful arabesques of white wrought iron and cushioned by needlepoint pillows with "Home Sweet Home," "Forget Hell!" and "You might be a Yankee if...," worked into the design—and seated within spittin' distance of a garden overflowing with blossoms—I was enjoying much the same life as had my grandmother. Perhaps the only difference between us would be that instead of sneaking sips of her husband's Mint Julep when no one was looking, I was quite openly enjoying a delightful Merlot in no one's company but my own.

A cool evening breeze wafted from the direction of the meadow carrying with it the delicate fragrance of wild honeysuckle and Carolina jasmine that grew in abundance on the fence separating pasture and lawn. Even the family of rabbits nibbling on red clover underneath the pear trees seemed to notice the sweetness in the air—every so often they raised their fuzzy, long-eared little heads and sniffed appreciatively.

Too bad, I thought as I poured another glass of wine, that I cannot relax and enjoy a quiet evening on my own patio. I had tried to shut my mind to the raucous shouts and screams coming from behind the carriage house and down the lane, but it was hopeless. No matter how delicious the wine, or how cute the bunnies, I was still annoyed.

I took another sip and cursed my mother's generosity for the umpteenth time since the soccer game began at four o'clock. When the Rowan Springs Wildkittens called two weeks ago and begged for a place to hold their matches, Mother's first inclination had been to say no; but then the desperate mother in charge of the team had explained that it was for the sake of twelve adorable little girls—aged eight to eleven years old—and Mother didn't have the heart to refuse.

At first, I didn't give it a second thought. Let the little darlings play their hearts out was my reaction. The field was going to be planted with soybeans in the fall. Surely whatever small amount of damage done by twenty-four girlish little feet would be of no consequence. I forgot about the superhuman strength of girlish vocal cords. Each child, I was positive, had the ability to break an eardrum at a hundred paces simply by screaming, "Goal!" at the top of her lungs. They had been at it now for about an hour, and I was ready to take Mother's John Deere and manically mow them down.

And this was just the first game.

"My! They do seem to be having fun!" observed Mother pleasantly, as she joined me on the patio. Her smile, as she offered a slice of roasted garlic crostini from a tray full of similar goodies, was almost as irritating as the noise. I told her so.

"Paisley Sterling! You are becoming quite the grouch these days. What's the matter, dear? Having trouble with your manuscript?"

Like most mothers, mine always knew exactly what to say to alter the course of a conversation, change the target of my frustrations, and get my goat.

"The latest Leonard Paisley is coming along just fine, thank you very much!" I answered with some asperity.

Her response was a loud and disapproving sigh—a sigh obviously meant to convey her opinion of the hard-boiled detective hero of the mystery series I wrote for a considerably good living. Mother had been after me for months to forego Leonard's dark and murky world of pimps and drug dealers and write about what she termed "more pleasant subjects." She blamed my mental association with Leonard for my somewhat earthy turn of phrase and casual manner of dress. I had news for her: since my daughter, Cassie, and I returned to Meadowdale Farm three years ago, I had thrown away my pantyhose and high-heeled shoes—as well as my desire to impress anyone, including my own mother.

The Poisoned Pen, by E. Joan Sims

Cassie and I had lived in Manhattan for too many years after we barely escaped the bloody coup that ravaged our home in San Romero. We left that beautiful South American country shortly after my husband, Raphael DeLeon, disappeared into the jungle on our wedding anniversary, an apparent victim of that same revolution.

Cassie and I had sought refuge in the welcoming home of my college roommate. Already well established as a literary agent, Pamela Winslow was the one who suggested I take up writing as a means of supporting myself and my little girl.

After several years as a successful author of children's books, I changed direction and took the long dark path down the road to murder and mayhem with the fictitious Leonard Paisley. Leonard was an overnight sensation. The revenue from his wild adventures gave me the financial freedom to bid farewell to the big city and return to my roots.

Cassie and I loved the small town of Rowan Springs, Kentucky. She even came back here after college to open a small and thriving bookstore. We were both as happy as clams. I saw no reason to change the *status quo,* and that included Leonard.

"Tart, dear?"

"Yes, you are, a bit," I responded with a lazy smile, "but I don't mind." Mother's delicious food was enough to calm any beast, and I was feeling a bit more mellow. I swallowed a flaky country ham and cheese pastry, and reached for more; but she had other ideas.

"If you insist on wearing those plebeian clothes, Paisley, darling, then perhaps you might at least shop for some jeans that fit. The ones you have on are looking indecently tight in the *derriere.* Have you put on some weight, dear?"

My appetite fled in the direction of my good humor and I sought once again to disengage myself from my surroundings by closing my eyes and pretending I was all alone.

"Hallo, Miz Sterling," interrupted an adenoidal little voice.

I opened my eyes to see a skinny, disheveled little girl of about nine standing shyly at the edge of the patio. She was wearing a bright yellow shirt, blue satin shorts, scuffed shin guards, and the muddiest tennis shoes I had ever seen. Her face was freckled and tan from the summer sun, with pale blue eyes and thin lips which held the faintest promise of a smile in the corners.

"I'm a Wildkitten—you know, the soccer team," she explained unnecessarily as she held out a large envelope—its edges soiled and covered with enough dirty fingerprints to drive Sherlock Holmes insane. "Thank you for letting us use your field," she said. "It's real nice." Then she turned and ran, scattering terrified bunnies in her wake.

"What a dear little thing," murmured Mother, holding the grimy card carefully by two dainty fingertips. "And what a sweet thought. Here," she said tossing the envelope in my direction, "you read it to me, dear."

"Hummpf!" I muttered. "Looks like they could have washed their hands first." The greeting card was handmade—with crude, but charming, crayon outlines of twelve girls standing around the edge of a green field filled with rabbits and soccer balls. Off in the distance was our own big rambling home with all four chimneys smoking.

"I have to admit it's cute. Somebody's a real little artist. I wonder if it was the booger baby who brought this."

"Paisley! She did not have...well, what you said! Don't be rude."

"Then you finally do need glasses, Mother, if you didn't...."

"Gran!" called Cassie from the big screened-in porch on the back of the house. "Telephone. It's Mavis Madden. Shall I tell her you're busy, or do you feel up to talking to the old witch?"

"Honestly, Paisley," sputtered Mother. "I don't know what's come over you and Cassandra. I do believe you have both taken leave of all your good manners. I thought when you came back here to live you would remember the way your father and I brought you up; but you both seem to have regressed even more into those dreadfully sarcastic Yankee ways."

I laughed. I couldn't help it. Mother always chose to forget that she was just one little Mason-Dixon line removed from "those dreadful Yankees." Kentucky was not known as a border state because of its proximity to Mexico, or Canada. Only a few hundred miles separated us from our northern neighbors—some of whom had even graced our esteemed family tree. I especially liked to recall the sad tale of one great, great, great uncle who had made that short journey out of family loyalty during the Civil War, and ended up swinging by his neck on a lonesome oak for his trouble.

Ordinarily, Mother would have sought any excuse to avoid talking to Mavis Madden. She didn't think any more highly of the old busybody than Cassie did; but to teach us a lesson in "southern lady manners" she hurried to the phone. Cassie took her seat on the patio and chuckled as she related Mavis's latest bit of tattle.

"According to Rowan Springs's own unofficial town crier, William Budd is growing pot in his basement."

I sneaked a handful of Mother's pastries and popped one in my mouth before I replied. "And just...mmmm, yum...how did Mavis figure this out?"

Cassie poked around on the *hors d'oeuvre* tray, discarding capers and meticulously removing fresh dill sprigs from the open-faced smoked salmon sandwiches. "She saw him carrying sacks of manure and potting soil from his truck down through the cellar door."

Cassie licked her fingers and flicked a green peppercorn at a greedy blue jay whose appetite had overcome his natural caution. The bird caught her gift in mid-air and flew off to a branch in the chestnut tree to savor his bounty.

"Personally," confided my daughter, "I think Mr. Budd could use few tokes of pot."

"Cassie!"

"I know how you feel about drugs, Mom, but you have to admit there never was a more uptight soul in all the world than that poor little man. For goodness sakes," she asked, changing the subject, "why does Gran have to mess up perfectly delicious food with all of these silly peppercorns and capers?"

I smiled, remembering. "You're so like your father, Cassie."

"Am I really, Mom?" she asked softly. "How? Tell me, please."

She uncurled her long slim legs and came to sit by me on the chaise lounge. Her dark hair hung like a shiny curtain around the porcelain oval of her face—her almost-black, brown eyes sparkling under soft, sooty, eyelashes. "Tell me about when I was a little girl," she begged. For a fleeting moment I saw a much younger child in the arms of the handsome father whose memory she adored. Hot tears welled behind my eyelids, and I had to clear my throat before I spoke.

"We lived in a garden," I whispered. "Not so unlike this one—except that it was bigger, and yet smaller at the same time." I always began the story the same way, and Cassie knew it well.

"I know, I know," she laughed. "Bigger outside and smaller in the middle."

"Yes," I nodded, smiling. "In the center of the house was an open area—a tiled courtyard—filled with flowers and a fountain."

"Which tinkled merrily all day and all night."

"Hey, who's telling this story?"

"You, Mom," she laughed, snuggling down next to me. "But don't forget the part about the parrots."

"Of course, not. That's the best...."

"Paisley!" shouted Mother in a shrill voice from the porch. "Paisley, come quick! Oh, dear! Something dreadful has happened!"

CHAPTER TWO

Cassie and I raced side by side down the walk. She reached the porch door first, slamming it open for the both of us.

"Gran! Are you all right?" she cried.

Mother was holding the portable phone in a limp hand. Her face was almost as white as the pearls around her slender neck.

"Mother," I gasped. "What in the world?"

"That charming little girl—Nell Jane Bradley—the one who brought us the thank-you card—she has disappeared."

"Disappeared?" I whispered in a hoarse voice. "Where?"

"Don't be a goose, Paisley!" answered Mother, her voice sharp with worry. "If we knew that, then the child wouldn't be missing!"

My stomach was doing flip-flops—ham and cheese pastries churned around and around in a sea of peppercorn acid. I had to swallow hard to keep from vomiting, and the sour aftertaste made me even more nauseous.

"You okay, Mom? You look a little green around the gills."

"I...I'm fine. It's just that...."

I made it to the sink in the nick of time.

"Cassandra, don't stand there with your mouth open. Hand your mother a damp towel. I'll make some tea."

"Tell me more, Mother," I asked, when I had swabbed my face and rinsed my mouth.

"Very well. If you don't ask any more silly questions."

I bit my tongue and let her continue in her own roundabout way.

"I was talking to Mavis. Well, actually, I was trying to get out of talking to Mavis, when the phone made that annoying beeping sound."

"Call waiting," I prompted.

"Yes! Well, you know how I feel about that rude bit of business."

"Yes, Gran. We know you never answer 'call waiting'," sighed Cassie. "That's why I never have a date."

"Yeah, right!" I laughed weakly, eager to throw off my sense of foreboding. We also knew that my daughter was so particular where men were concerned that even Prince Charming would have to submit a resume.

"Well, it is rude," insisted Mother. "But this time it was unrelenting and I had to answer to put a stop to it. One of the soccer mothers was on the other line. She said that Nell Jane never returned from delivering the card to us. The others waited for a few minutes, then went to look for her. When the search turned up nothing, they called for help. The woman wanted to warn us that the police and the emergency medical crew would be using our driveway to get back to the field where the children were playing."

At that moment we heard the swift crunch of gravel as Chief Andy Joiner's police cruiser and two more like it raced up the drive and down pass the carriage house towards the lane. They were followed closely by the ambulance and the Lakeland County EMS.

"Well, thanks for the warning, Mother," I said, sarcastically. "It's a good thing Watson wasn't in the driveway!" Watson was my bilious green Jeep Cherokee—my pride and joy.

"Or Aggie!" Cassie added. "She would have been squashed! By the way, where is Aggie? I haven't seen her for hours."

Agatha Christie, Aggie for short, was Cassie's ill-tempered Lhasa Apso. The dog was almost four years old now, but she hadn't mellowed one little bit with age. In fact, she was even more evil than the benighted day Cassie when picked her out from the rest of her littermates and brought her to live with us. The dog was cute—of that there could be no doubt. She was white and soft, and as fuzzy as a cotton ball; but she didn't like being touched, moved, nudged, or reprimanded. She had bitten me each and every time I had done any one of the above.

Aggie could usually be found in the middle of my bed on

my favorite down pillow. Cassie knew that, but I reminded her, anyway.

"We all have to make sure our own little chicks are okay," said Mother with a sad smile, as she watched Cassie rush off to my bedroom. "Maybe I'll call your sister tonight. We haven't talked for two weeks."

"Right!" I laughed—glad for the sound and feel of it. "She could have gotten married and divorced at least twice in two weeks."

"Paisley! Don't be so unpleasant. You should rejoice that Velvet appears to have finally found happiness."

"Found it again, you mean! Let's see—is Harry Mason Biddle III Velvet's number four, or number five? I can't keep them straight. I hope she can."

Mother secretly agreed with me, I was almost positive, but she never liked to show even a whit of favoritism. She changed the subject without batting an eyelash.

"Are you going back in the field, dear?"

"I was considering it, but I don't want to get in the way of the police."

"I think you should, Paisley. Perhaps you could help with the children. Take them something to eat, or...."

"Just a minute, Mother! The kids are still back there? Why in the blue-eyed world haven't they gone home? Aren't their parents worried sick?"

"The woman who called me said Andy Joiner wanted everyone to stay exactly where they were until he got there."

I didn't want to go. I didn't even want to think about it. When Cassie was small I used to wake up in the wee small hours, sweating and terrified that she had gone missing like her father.

"I'll go," I sighed. "Do you have some sweet tea or lemonade in the fridge? That might help. And maybe some cookies."

Mother smiled and patted my hand. "Yes, dear. I'll have everything ready in a minute. Perhaps Cassie would like to keep you company. You two make a good team."

I found Cassie curled up on my bed with the nasty little puppy asleep in her arms. She was crying softly into the dog's furry neck.

"Oh, darling, don't cry! They'll find her." I lay down next

15

to her and stroked her hair. Aggie raised her sleepy head and bared her upper teeth. I got out of the way a second before she lunged and snapped—missing my fingers by barely an inch. Cassie stopped crying and began to laugh.

"Oh, Mom!" she gasped. "You should have seen the look on your face!"

"Damn, damn, and double damn! That rotten little beast!"

"Mom!"

"Okay," I sighed. "If it makes you happy—the stinking little...."

"Mom...."

"Okay," I smiled. "She can bite me anytime." Nevertheless, I placed the other pillow carefully between me and Aggie before I sat back down. "Gran is fixing some lemonade and cookies for me to take to the soccer kiddies and their moms. Want to go with?"

"Sure," she smiled, wiping away the tears.

"Bad memories, Cassie?" I asked, unsure as to how far I should go.

"Yeah. You know—Daddy and everything." She looked out the big bay window, watching the fireflies dance in the deepening twilight before she continued. "I was always so afraid that you would vanish the same way he did," she said in a voice hoarse with more unshed tears.

"Looks like each of us was afraid of the same thing. We should have had this little talk long before now. It might have saved us both a lot of sleepless nights." I squeezed her hand as I made a promise. "I love you, kitten, and I'll never, ever, go anywhere without leaving you a forwarding address." I started to hug her, but Aggie gave another deep, throaty, warning growl so I settled for a big, noisy, kiss in the air instead. "Ready to go play Clara Barton?"

"Clara Barton...now, don't tell me. She's the *femme fatale* with the famous lips who starred in the early silent films. Right?"

"Cassie, Clara Barton was...."

"No! Let me guess. You're always pulling these old movie stars out of a hat. You have to give me time to think. Westerns? Was she in that western with Harry Cooper?"

CHAPTER THREE

With some difficulty Cassie and I carried a large cooler filled to the brim with ice and several jugs of sweet tea and lemonade to my Jeep. We chucked it inside and carefully loaded the two large tins of homemade cookies Mother had packed.

"Come back for more tea if you run out, dear. I'm afraid I don't have any more cookies, but I can come up with something else if need be."

"Thanks, Mother, but I'm sure the kid's already been found by now. How far could she go, anyway?"

"Not very far on her own, dear; but that doesn't seem to be the concern."

"Oh."

My thoughts returned to dark and gloomy as Cassie and I bounced down the lane that led to the backfield. The green eyes that stared back at me from Watson's rear view mirror were cloudy with concern, and my face was so pale even the freckles had disappeared. "Do you really think there is anyone in Lakeland County who's mean enough to kidnap a little girl?"

"Give me a break, Mom! I love living here. Who wouldn't? But you have to admit we have out share of weirdoes."

"Yeah, but eccentric weirdoes—like Mr. Budd, or Dora Nick, or even Horatio Raleigh"

"Horatio? Why, Horatio? Because he's been in love with Gran for the last five decades?"

"That, too; but I was thinking it was because he's the only ex-member of a clandestine government intelligence operation who's managed to turn funerals into an art form."

"Very funny, Mom."

"Well, I'm trying."

Horatio Raleigh had been a friend of my family for years. He and Mother had gone to school together, and he had always had a crush on her. When my father came to live in Rowan Springs after the war—and stole my mother's heart, Horatio had graciously stepped aside. He remained at a loyal and respectful distance until two years after John Sterling passed away, then resumed his courtship.

I was fairly certain that my mother would never marry again, but Horatio refused to give up hope. He turned the funeral home over to his nephew and spent his days cheerfully doing Mother's bidding. Only the passing of a dear friend, or the offer of an exorbitant fee for his "special consultation" could draw him out of retirement. I was glad for his constant attentions to my mother because he made her happy; but I also loved the old man, and I prized his expert opinion on many things.

Watson burst out of the shadowy tunnel of the lane and into the open field beyond. The going was a lot rougher as we bounced over furrows—tall grass slapping at the windscreen and showering us with seeds. And it was getting darker with every passing minute.

"Mom! For Pete's sake! You're shaking my fillings loose."

"Oh, sorry, honey. I'll slow down."

"You don't fool me at all! This is exactly why you wanted to buy Watson in the first place. You're having the time of your life!"

Andy Joiner had parked his cruiser with the headlights shining towards the tangled thicket at the end of the soccer field. Dad had built us a tree house in that woodsy glen when Velvet and I were children—when it wasn't so overgrown. Later, he insisted that the forest remain in its natural state so that the animals—deer, rabbits, and foxes would have a place to forage and raise their young. I still remembered every inch of the place we called "the jungle." If Nell Jane were lost in there, I would be the perfect candidate to go in after her.

"But, damn it, Andy! I spent half my childhood playing Tarzan in that thicket! And to tell you the truth," I said, lowering my voice, "your deputies are a little too porky to go crawling around under those vines. Now, I could...."

"Paisley, you know perfectly well that I can't let a civilian take part in a potentially hazardous police investigation."

"Then deputize me! I'll be the best deputy you've ever had! Please, Andy, please!"

"Well, I don't know," he said, scratching his head, then rolling his hat brim nervously his big hands. "We're not real sure of what we're dealing with here."

"One thing's for certain—a frightened little girl is lost and we're wasting valuable time hemming and hawing."

"Okay," he sighed. "Raise your right hand and repeat after me."

Thirty minutes later I was bitterly regretting my insistence on becoming Lakeland County's newest public servant. My hair was full of twigs and leaves, and my face scratched and burning where I had brushed against vines and stinging nettles. I had crawled on my hands and knees, slithered on my belly, and fought my way through the dense underbrush with nothing but the flashlight Andy had given me.

"My kingdom for a machete!" I gasped, as I wiped the sweat off my face and plucked a burr from behind my ear. A lot of years had passed since I last played under the low limbs of the willow and sassafras growing in wild profusion in our jungle. I hated to admit it, but I had lost all sense of direction. Blackberry, scuppernong, and honeysuckle vines wound around every tree and bush and filled all of the spaces in between. I felt like I was tangled up inside a big prickly ball of yarn.

I tried to stand, but there wasn't any room. My head struck the low hanging limb of a cedar and something with too many legs scurried across my hand as I rubbed the tender spot. Tears of frustration and anger filled my eyes. Andy Joiner would never let me forget it, but I had to confess that I was licked.

I was turning around to go back the way I came when I heard a small snuffling sound off to my left.

"Nell Jane?" I called softly. "Honey, is that you?"

The crying increased, but there was no answer. I crawled forward, calling softly so as not to frighten the child even more.

"Nell Jane, sweetheart, it's Paisley Sterling. You know me, honey. Why, just this afternoon you gave me a beautiful card. I bet you made that card didn't you?"

"Ye...yes," called a hesitant little voice over the tears.

"Well, you are quite an artist. Your mother must be very proud of you."

The crying increased in both volume and tempo, but the little girl refused to respond to any more of my questions. Thorns tore at my clothes and caught at my hair as I made my way toward her. I swore viciously when I put my hand down on something quick and slimy, and apologized to the child automatically. I was rewarded by a tiny little laugh.

"That's the ticket," I told her. "Laugh at me all you want. Can you see my flashlight? Am I getting close?"

"Yes," she answered. "You're all dirty."

I pointed the flashlight in the direction of her voice and saw the child clinging to the trunk of a small sassafras. She didn't look any better than I did. Her shirt was torn and every bare inch of her skin was crisscrossed with scratches. Somewhere she had lost her shorts, and her legs looked thin and vulnerable sticking out of her little white cotton panties.

"Hi, Nell Jane," I said, with what I hoped was a reassuring smile. "It's nice to see you again."

Later, I couldn't remember how I got us out of the jungle; but I do know I left a good bit of my hide and several hunks of hair behind. I handed the little girl over to the paramedics and stumbled toward Watson and my own distraught child.

"Mom! Oh, my God! What have you done to yourself?"

Cassie took off her sweater and wrapped it around my shoulders. It wasn't until I felt its warmth that I realized I was shivering.

"You should let one of the paramedics check you out, Mom," she insisted.

"No. I just want to go home. A bath is all I need—a nice warm bath."

Cassie helped me in the Jeep and gave me a quick hug. She had turned the car around to head for home when Andy came running over in front of Watson waving his arms.

"Paisley!" he called. "You were right. Thanks for finding her." He took a closer look at me under the harsh glare of the emergency lights. "I need to ask you some questions, but it can wait." He started to walk away, and turned back. "You really ought'a see one of the paramedics, you know."

"I'm fine, Andy," I assured him. "See you later."

Cassie drove slowly and carefully over the bumpy field. As we got farther and farther away from the ring of emergency vehicles, the darkness seemed to devour us.

I leaned back in the seat and took a deep breath—sighing as I exhaled.

"Are you sure you're okay, Mom?"

"Well, let's see," I answered, taking stock. "I have bump as big as a goose egg on my head. My favorite jeans are ruined. I crawled through a big old patch of poison ivy. And I think I swallowed a spider, but other then that, I'm just hunky-dory."

"You're a hero, you know," said my daughter, with a proud smile.

"Big whoop."

CHAPTER FOUR

The hot bath felt even better than I had imagined. I lathered up twice and rinsed off, then filled the tub again for a long soak in the sweet, oil-scented water. My hair, however, presented a more difficult problem. In the past few weeks I had let it get too long and the tight auburn curls were frizzy and difficult to brush out under the best of conditions. Tonight I had no choice but to resort to the scissors.

It wasn't the first time I had cut my own hair. I hated beauty parlors. To my mind they were full of noxious odors, silly women, and malicious gossip. I avoided them like the plague.

Reluctantly, I left the warm, sweet-scented haven of my bathroom and wrapped up in a long terry robe. Mother and Cassie were out on the back porch with their heads together over the remainder of my bottle of wine and a big tray of cheese and fruit.

"Oh, dear!" apologized Mother. "I'm afraid we've finished off your wine, Paisley, dear. Shall I open another, or would you like something else?"

"Water's fine, Mother." I showed her the bottle I had grabbed from the fridge on my way out. "I would like a hunk of that funny-smelling cheese, though, and some grapes."

"Cassie, please cut your mother a slice of *manchego* with the cheese knife before she disfigures it with her fork."

"Cut her some slack, Gran. Mom's had quite a night."

"Nonsense! She was simply fulfilling her civic duty. Anyone would have done as much. Although," she added, as she leaned over and rewarded me with a quick kiss on the cheek, "I'm sure our Paisley did it with more panache." She paused and looked at me closely in the dim light of the citronella candle. "What have you done with your hair?"

"Oh, Mom, what have you done?" giggled Cassie. "You look like...."

"Please, don't say Raggedy Ann," I begged.

"I was thinking more of the Chia pet my roommate had at Emory."

I jerked the hood of my robe up over my head and grumbled, "Never mind my hair. I'm a writer, not a model, for goodness sake."

"Yes, but...."

"But, what, Mother?" I demanded.

"Beth Davis called from the *Rowan Springs Gazette* to ask for an interview with the heroine of the day."

"And you refused, I hope!"

"No, dear, I'm afraid not. As a matter of fact, I invited her for breakfast. You're usually at your best in the morning."

"Damn, damn, and double damn! I hate that silly twit! She couldn't write her way out of a paper sack."

"You have to admit she's entertaining, Mom. Remember the wedding we were reading about last week. Describing a fifty-pound wedding cake shaped like a guitar in a hundred words or less can't be all that easy."

"She's pedantic and obtuse—and what's worse, she's a literary snob! Can you imagine anyone in Rowan Springs understanding her constant references to the bride and groom as Beatrice and Benedick?"

"Of course, dear."

"Why am I surprised that you disagree with me, Mother?" I asked with a shake of my shorn curls. "And by the way, why do you?"

"Miss Davis and quite a few of her peers were students of your father's before he retired. Shakespeare's comedies were required reading in his English Literature classes, and *Much Ado About Nothing* was one of his favorites. I'm sure some people are quite well-acquainted with Beatrice and Benedick."

Mother had taken some of the wind out of my sails, but I refused to admit defeat. "Well, I still don't want her here. She's always trying to get me to read her latest attempt at the great American novel. Last week I had to duck into the feed store and hide behind the Bag Balm shelf for twenty minutes until she finally quit gabbing with some poor soul and went on her merry way. I've managed to avoid her for months and now my very own mother has invited her into the bosom of my family!"

Mother straightened her shoulders and zoomed in for the kill. "Be kind, Paisley, dear," she ordered quietly. "More cheese?"

Mother went to bed early, but Cassie and I made ourselves comfortable on the lounges and listened to the frogs and crickets until almost midnight.

"Aren't you exhausted, Mom?"

"You'd think so, wouldn't you? But I love hearing the night songs of all those little creatures. It's is one of the things I missed the most when we lived in the city."

"I love the sound, too," she agreed. "But I hate the thought of all that unrequited love."

"Lonesome, Cassie?"

"Absolutely not! You may not believe it, Mom, but I practically have to beat 'em off with a stick!"

I smiled in the darkness as I conjured up a picture of my tall, slender, and very beautiful daughter fending off hordes of hopeful and insistent swain. "Is there no one in Rowan Springs worthy of your charming company?" I teased.

"Maybe a couple, but they're married."

"You're kidding! Who are they?"

"Bruce Hawkins for one."

"He comes on to you?" I was surprised and disappointed. Bruce was Mother's lawyer. I really liked and respected him, and his wife was one of the few people in Rowan Springs I wanted to get to know better.

"No," she answered, thoughtfully. "I don't think you could call it that, but he has been spending a lot of time in the bookstore lately. Then again, Mary usually meets him there after work, and they always seem really happy to see one another. She's getting a little chubby," Cassie added, with a smile. "I think she might be pregnant."

"Well, then you can forget about Mr. Hawkins. Who's the other one?"

"William Budd."

"Good grief, Cassie! That funny little man? Whatever do you see in him?"

"He's sweet," she protested. "And if he lost the granny glasses and changed his wardrobe a bit he could be really interesting looking."

"Maybe so...but somehow I think his neck would fall off if he didn't wear that bow tie."

"Don't be mean, Mom."

I cleared my throat of the chuckle that was threatening. "You said married men. Is Budd married?"

"He wasn't married for very long. His wife died last year," she said softly.

"Oh! Sorry. Who was she? Anyone I might know?"

"I never heard her name before. I think she was someone he met when he went away to school. She was ill for several years. He's not as old as you think. He's just had a hard time."

"My God, Cassie! You sound like you've fallen for this character."

"No, Mom," she stated firmly. "But I do enjoy his conversation, and I can hardly ask one of my best customers to quit coming around."

"But he's old! He almost as old as...."

"You, Mom?" asked Cassie, barely suppressing her laughter. "He did mention that he had a crush on you when you were in junior high."

"See! He's just a year, or two...."

"No, Mom," she laughed. "He was six, and you were his baby sitter."

I slept late the next morning—or at least, I pretended to. For the last couple of years I had managed to arrange my life just to suit me. Perhaps I was spoiled, but I liked having the freedom to decide what I wanted to do and when I wanted to do it. I deeply resented any unwanted changes in my schedule.

When Cassie rapped sharply on my door, I turned over and buried my head under the pillow. "Rats, rats, rats," I mumbled angrily. "I should have left that snot-nosed little brat in the jungle."

"Now, now, Mom, you don't really mean that," admonished Cassie, as she entered my room and sat down on the edge of my bed. Aggie's toenails clicked rapidly on the bare wood floors as she ran to join her mistress.

"Go away! I'm asleep! And take that rotten little beast

with you. She's been burying dog biscuits under my pillow again. I had to get up twice during the night just to brush the crumbs off my sheets."

"Come on, Mom. Miss Davis is here—all bright and shiny as a new copper penny. Looks like she bought an outfit just for this interview. She must really think you're something special!"

"Then fill her in on the story of the 'real me,' and tell her to buzz off."

"Gran's loving all of the attention you're getting," she said, trying a new tactic. "She'll be very disappointed if you're not on the front page of tomorrow's paper."

I turned over and sat up, propping my pillows behind me. I took the cup of hot tea Cassie had brought me and winked at her.

"Then she's forgotten that old southern adage: a lady's name appears in print only twice—when she marries and when she dies."

"Get dressed, Mom. They're waiting for you on the patio."

CHAPTER FIVE

Cassie and Aggie had rejoined Mother and her guest by the time I slipped on my favorite sweats and old beat-up Cole-Haan moccasins. Last year, after a tornado had cut a swath through our town, Mother took advantage of the situation and cleaned out my closet on the pretext of helping those who had lost everything in the storm. It took me three weeks, but I finally found what I was looking for at the Salvation Army store. In return for a generous donation, I managed to retrieve my comfortable "oldies but goodies" and return them to their rightful place in my wardrobe. I wore them on those special occasions when I wanted to make Mother mad enough to lose her cool.

It worked—almost. Her patrician features, as she watched me walk out to the patio, registered her disapproval, but her words were those of any proud mother.

"Here comes my darling daughter, now," she announced, with a strained smile. "Paisley, you remember Bethlehem Davis."

"Bethlehem? I don't remember that!"

The reporter managed to laugh at what must have been a very tiresome reaction to her unusual name after thirty-something years. The laughter sounded okay; but I noticed her eyes weren't involved—pale brown, almost amber, they were narrowed against the sunlight in a round face with flat cheekbones and a little pug nose. Her faded brown hair was pulled back in a limp ponytail and adorned with tired artificial daisies and a paper butterfly. Beth Davis appeared nervous and ill at ease, even though—and perhaps because—Mother was trying her best to make her feel at home.

"Are you sure you won't have another biscuit, Beth, dear?

More ham?"

Cassie was right—Beth did have on a new outfit. A little round "inspected by #23" sticker still clung to the hem of her bright yellow and orange flowered dress. Her liberal use of Crayola colors and her plain, flat features brought to mind a cartoon character, but for the life of me I couldn't figure out which one.

"I'll have a biscuit, Mother," I said, as I flopped unceremoniously down on the chaise, "and stuff it, please."

"I beg your pardon?" she asked, raising one elegantly curved eyebrow.

I winked at Cassie—only to receive a warning glare from my daughter in return. "Please put a slice of ham inside, thank you, Mother," I sighed, deciding there would be hell to pay later if I didn't act at least a little civilized now. I got some hell, anyway.

"I've been telling Bethlehem about your daring rescue of little Nell Jane, Paisley. Do you have anything to add to the story before you change into something more appropriate for your photograph?"

Beth had me pose under the magnolia, on top of the old well, and finally, on the white wrought iron bench in my moon garden. The last picture was a favor for me. My beautiful, newly landscaped moon garden with its heirloom white roses and all white flowers was a private place, and not for prying eyes.

With Mother out of the way, Beth loosened up and we actually had a rather pleasant conversation—especially pleasant for me because she had read and enjoyed all of Leonard's books.

"He's such a devil, that man! He frightens me—and yet, thrills me at the same time!" she confided in a voice full of barely suppressed excitement. "You have such a command of the English language, Paisley. You're a veritable magician of the imagination, truly a conjurer...."

"Yeah, yeah," I said, stopping her from digging any deeper into her mental thesaurus.

A faint blushed stained her plain cheeks, making her briefly more attractive. "Sorry," she mumbled apologetically, "I do tend to go on when I wax enthusiastic."

I felt instantly contrite. For some strange reason, I was beginning to like this young woman, and not just because she admired me.

"How's your own book coming along?" I asked, biting my tongue so I wouldn't say more than I intended.

Two hours later, I stood by her car holding four pounds of tattered manuscript bound together by several thick rubber bands and waiting impatiently for her to leave.

"Oh, Paisley! You don't know how much this means to me—to have you, a true word smith—a laudable literary lion—reading, nay critiquing, my puny efforts!"

I sighed deeply, trying to maintain the semblance of a smile. My warm feelings for Bethlehem Davis were rapidly turning tepid. "Don't expect feedback any time soon," I warned her sourly. "I'm...."

"I know! I know!" she cried gaily. "Busy, busy, busy! But just being able to think that you are the temporary caretaker of my tome gives me such a thrill! You'll never know how much I appreciate this." She pointed to the first page of fully packed, single-spaced sentences. "I do hope it isn't too hard on your eyes. We poor aspiring young novelists have to save on paper, you know."

"And printer ink, too, I noticed."

She smiled and blew me a kiss as she turned her little yellow Volkswagen bug around in the drive and headed out to the highway. I had started up the walk when I heard her slam on the brakes and back up rapidly, scattering gravel in her wake.

"Paisley!" she called.

"Oh, God! What now?" I muttered, turning around with a forced smile.

She leaned out of the car window, an earnest inquiring look on her face. "I almost forgot to ask you," she called out. "Did that little girl say anything to you about a strange man in the woods?"

I walked back to her car so I wouldn't have to yell. "What man?" I asked.

"I went out to the Bradley's house last night to get an interview for the paper. Mrs. Bradley wouldn't let me talk to her daughter; but she told me that Nell Jane said a big man with a black beard and one eye chased her into the woods and took off her shorts. I just wondered if the child said anything like that to you."

I tried to keep the surprise from showing on my face, but apparently didn't succeed.

"I was astounded, too," Beth agreed. "But the mother was very insistent—and angry that the authorities weren't taking the child's story seriously. She threatened to call the FBI if Chief Joiner didn't investigate more thoroughly!"

"Can I give you an answer off the record, Beth?"

"Well...I'm not supposed to suppress the news."

"This isn't news," I sighed.

"Okay, then. Just this once—for you—I promise!" she said, raising her hand and then crossing her heart with her fingers. "Cross my heart, and hope to...."

"Yeah, yeah," I interrupted. I still didn't trust her enough to protect my privacy, so I chose my words very carefully. "It was dark, and the little girl was terrified. Crawling out of that thicket and finding half the town and every squad car in the county must have scared her even more. She probably felt she had to place the blame for causing so much trouble on someone other than herself—when the truth is—she probably got lost chasing a rabbit into the brush. I find it hard to believe her story."

"Me, too!" declared Beth. "But her mother sure is running with it. I feel sorry for that child when the truth comes out. Mrs. Bradley seems to be a 'spare the rod and spoil the child' type of parent."

"Is there a Mr. Bradley?" I asked curiously.

"Instead of answering, she quickly consulted the old-fashioned bracelet watch on her right wrist. "Must be off," she announced abruptly. "Thanks a bunch, Paisley!"

I watched her head down the drive and turn into the highway; almost wishing she would come back so I could ask some questions of my own.

"What's in that package, Mom?" asked Cassie with a sly smile as I opened the screened door to the back porch. "Don't tell me the redoubtable Miss Bethlehem Davis finally convinced you to read her masterpiece?"

I threw the hefty packet in the corner—and watched in dismay as the rubber bands popped and the manuscript exploded into a small mushroom-shaped cloud.

"Good job!" observed Cassie. "I hope for your sake the pages were numbered, Mom."

"Oh, my God! Surely she had the good sense...thank heavens!" I swore in relief as I picked up a handful of pages and looked them over. "What a mess!"

"Are you really going to read it?"

I sat down at table and started sorting out the pages. "I guess so, I promised—even though I had no choice, thanks to Mother."

"Thanking me, dear?" asked Mother, as she joined us. "Whatever for? Not that there aren't many things for which you should show your appreciation."

"Well," I said with a wicked grin, "then perhaps I should begin by letting you have first go at Bethlehem's manuscript."

"That's lovely of you, Paisley. I think I just might take you up on that."

"You will?"

"Why, of course! Miss Davis is quite an interesting young woman. She could use some guidance in her style of dress, but she's headed in the right direction. At least she has the good sense to eschew jeans in favor of a skirt. Yes, I think our Miss Davis has possibilities. I would definitely like to explore the world of her imagination. After all, I do so enjoy her articles in the Gazette. Her *chef d'oeuvre* could prove very enlightening."

"Well, here then!" I declared petulantly, plopping the hodge-podge of pages down in front of her.

"Where are you going, dear?" called Mother, as I slammed the porch door and headed for the carriage house.

"The Dairy Queen!" I shouted over my shoulder. "What's it to ya'?" I muttered angrily under my breath.

CHAPTER SIX

The Diary Queen out on Highway 62 was Rowan Springs's favorite fast food eatery—the truth is—it was the only fast food joint in town. When I arrived at half past noon I saw the drive-thru lane was already filled with a stream of hungry and impatient office workers. Cursing my luck, I drove around to the back searching for a parking spot and spotted Horatio Raleigh's big silver Bentley stationed majestically aloof at the far end.

I placed my order at the counter, then squeezed my way through the crowd to a quiet corner in the back. Always the gentleman, Horatio stood and bowed slightly, gesturing for me to sit opposite him in the booth.

"Congratulations, my dear!" he said, raising his chocolate malt in salutation. "I understand you are the woman of the hour."

"Hopefully fame will prove to be as fleeting as they claim!" I answered ruefully. "So far, it's brought me nothing but a peck of trouble."

"Your mother told me about the upcoming article in the Gazette. I suppose that is the trouble to which you are referring?"

"Yep! Not only do I have to suffer the invasion of my well-deserved privacy by having my photograph plastered all over tomorrow's early edition, but I also have to read fourteen-hundred and fifty-two pages of a single-spaced, barely legible autobiography written by a thirty-three year old spinster with no life."

"Oh, my! That is a fate worse than death," he chuckled.

"Don't get me wrong," I explained. "Beth Davis seems to be a very nice person. She's articulate—maybe a little too articulate—and smart; but that doesn't always add up to talent. Look at me! I'm not that smart, and according to Mother, I'm practically tongue-tied."

"And yet you are the successful novelist Miss Davis aspires to be. Did anyone extend a helping hand on your road to success, Paisley?"

"Why, of course! Pam, my agent, helped me do everything; but you know that, Horatio." I looked up and saw the chiding look on his handsome, aristocratic face. "Oh, I see—I'm being a spoiled rotten brat again, aren't I?"

"Certainly not now that you're aware of your fall from grace," he answered with a smile.

"Oh, well," I sighed. "I guess you're right. I'll read it when Mother finishes."

A short, plump woman in a Dairy Queen uniform walked up to our table. "Miz DeLeon. I have your order."

"Goodness! I would have come to the counter if you had called me," I protested.

"Well, I wanted to thank you in person for what you done last night."

I looked carefully, but didn't see any of Nell Jane's thin, sharp, features in the woman's broad face and stout body. "Are you related to the little girl?" I asked.

"No, no," she laughed. "I'm Darlene Hanson—Tiffany's mother. But I was there last night. Those little girls was mighty upset until Nell Jane got found. It would'a killed them if that man had made off with her."

"Did you see the man?" I asked curiously.

The two little half-moons she had drawn above her eyes with a cheap black makeup pencil came together as she tried to remember. "Maybe.... It was dark, ya' know. I thought I saw a man's shadow just on the far side of the goal—so did Tiffany, and a couple of the other little girls." She smiled sadly. "They're so scared now—I guess they'll wanna do all their practicing in the morning. Tiffany may even have to drop off the team unless I can swap hours with somebody on the night shift."

Darlene gave me a quick pat on the shoulder. "Anyway, thanks again," she said, and hurried back to the front. I unwrapped my cheeseburger and took a bite while I reflected on her words. Horatio seemed to be doing the same thing.

"Very interesting," he observed. "Mass hysteria would not be an uncommon phenomenon under the circumstances—a group of prepubescent females worked into a frenzy by the physical stresses of a highly emotional game—suddenly one of their own vanishes. It would be devastating."

"She wandered off after a bunny, Horatio," I mumbled over a mouthful of fries.

He made careful packets of his burger wrappers and folded them on the tray, then pulled a spotless linen handkerchief from his pocket and wiped his hands.

"You saw the child first, Paisley. At least, that's my understanding. Is that what she told you?"

"Well...no." I wadded my own waste papers in a messy ball and tossed them on the tray next to his. "I did most of the talking," I admitted. "But I was just trying to calm her down. She was pretty scared."

"Of a bunny?" he asked, raising his own immaculately groomed eyebrows.

"It was dark! And I don't mind telling you I was frightened, too. Geez, Horatio, there were snakes and worms and spiders in that thicket. It was a nine-year-old girl's worst nightmare!"

"There are worse things than spiders, worms, and snakes, Paisley."

"Worse than spiders?" I asked with a grin. "Not in my book!"

I tagged along behind my elegant friend as we made our way out of the busy restaurant. He paused to speak to several acquaintances while I shifted impatiently from one foot to another, aching to get out of the pressing crowd.

When two toddlers in the middle of a ketchup war plodded heedlessly over my toes in their teeny-weeny combat boots, I turned and ran for the nearest exit, vowing never again to indulge a salty grease attack at rush hour.

Horatio caught up with me as I was buckling up my seat belt.

"Sorry about that, my dear. In my business you never know when you're meeting a prospective customer. His Honor the Mayor, looked a trifle jaundiced, don't you think?"

"Horatio!"

"I thought that would make you smile!" He patted the edge of my window. "Nice buggy, your Watson. You know, I've never taken him out for a spin. Do you mind, Paisley?"

"You? Now?"

"Why not!" he declared. "No time like the present. Scoot over my dear, and let an old man have some fun."

I don't know what I expected—perhaps a tentative, meandering drive through the hills around the lake, but Horatio surprised me yet again. He climbed behind the wheel and took us on a silent, completely focused, and very fast roller-coaster ride which came to a screeching halt on the bluff overlooking the state penitentiary and the river down below.

"They call it the Castle on the Cumberland. Did you know that?" he asked, as he turned off the engine.

"Wha...what?" I gasped, trying to get my breath.

"Why, Paisley! Are you all right? You look positively ill. Too many French fries, perhaps?"

"Where did you learn to drive like that, Horatio? I'm still trying to catch up with my liver." I opened the car door and stumbled out. "I need some fresh air."

I staggered over to the small sandstone wall surrounding the edge of the cliff and sat down, swinging my legs over to the other side. The wall, intended to protect the foolish from getting too close to the edge, was used by young daredevils as a diving platform. The tumbling surface of the wide surging river was twenty windswept feet below.

The view across the Cumberland and into the valleys and fields beyond was spectacular. A hundred different shades of green—from pale celadon to dark greenish-blue—tinted a forest of trees in the distant hills. The fields were planted in a fertile patchwork of soybeans, sorghum, and corn—with a scattering of white farmhouses and red barns in between. Directly beneath us, dry yellow bulrushes and fuzzy brown cat's tails danced in the wind against the background of the mighty river.

"Mind if I smoke?" asked Horatio, as he spread a handkerchief on the wall and sat next to me.

"You know I love the smell of your pipe, Horatio. Can you really see two states from here?"

"I truly doubt it," he answered with a smile. "But the view

is breathtaking, nevertheless."

"Even the old prison is picturesque—if you squint your eyes and ignore all that shiny new barbed wire."

"That picturesque old prison is the present address of little Nell Jane Bradley's father."

"You're kidding!" I looked at the forbidding stone walls and tall gray towers with renewed interest. "That's why you brought me out here!"

"Yes," he admitted.

"Why the warp speed?"

He turned and grinned at me over his pipe stem. "Because I was having the time of my life. And because sometimes it's more meaningful to enjoy your own freedom to the fullest when you are about to encounter others who have lost theirs. I intend to drive back in the same 'hell bent for leather' fashion. If you'll let me, that is."

"Let you? Horatio, I'll hoot and holler with you. It must be awful to be locked up inside those thick stone walls. Uggh!" I shuddered "What did he do?"

"Bradley? I can't recall, exactly."

"Juvenile delinquent?"

"All of the old clichés," he said with a sad smile, as he puffed fragrant "O"s out over the river. "Impregnated his high school sweetheart, shotgun wedding, another baby on the way before the first was out of diapers, lost his job when the textile mill closed—drinking, carousing, in trouble with the law, and finally—jailed, leaving his uneducated, untrained wife to support three children on food stamps and hand-outs from her church—all the elements of one of your country western songs."

"Nell Jane seems bright," I observed hopefully. "And creative."

"Perhaps, too creative," he laughed. "Jake Bradley was a bright child, also. The Bradley's had a big tobacco farm—several hundred acres. Lemuel Bradley had big hopes for his only son, and he became quite a bitter man after Jake dropped out of high school to marry the Holster girl. When Lemuel's wife died, he sold the farm and left town. Nobody's heard from him since."

"Not even when his son got into trouble and went to

prison?"

"Sad, isn't it? Pride, as they say, goeth before...."

"Yeah, yeah," I grinned. "I'll do better, I promise."

Horatio tapped his pipe on the heel of his handmade Italian loafer, and smiled. "Not every homily is aimed at you, my dear," he observed.

"Just in case, Horatio, just in case."

CHAPTER SEVEN

I waved farewell to Horatio in the parking lot of the Dairy Queen and scooted over to take my place behind the wheel for a cautious drive home.

"Have fun, Mom?" asked Cassie, as I plopped down beside her on the front porch swing. "Enjoy your weekly self-indulgent intake of fat grams and calories?"

"I think I'm gonna puke again," I admitted, and told her about Horatio's wild ride through the hills. "And the most unbelievable thing of all was the way he enjoyed it so! I'd be willing to swear he winked at me when he said goodbye."

"Wow!" was her reply. "Is he great, or what? Where are all the young Horatios hiding these days?"

"I honestly don't think they're making them like that any more," I sighed.

The white wicker swing creaked pleasantly as we relaxed against the green and pink-checked cushions to enjoy the sweet afternoon breeze. It was still too early in June to get really hot, and the temperature was hovering in the comfortable mid-seventies.

I was pleased to see that the front yard had almost recovered from the aftermath of last year's tornado. The grass was as green and thick as ever. The surviving lilacs were blooming like crazy, and three small dogwoods and all the evergreen shrubs around the house were thriving. And to prove that all was well, several pairs of fat, red-breasted robins had returned with the spring and found ample spots for nest building.

"Nice, huh?"

"Umm," Cassie agreed in a lazy voice.

"We should sit out here more often."

"Umm."

"The birds are almost as much fun to watch as the bunnies."

"Umm."

I got up and lifted her feet into the swing. "Take a nap, Toots. I want to ask Mother a couple of questions."

"Good luck," murmured Cassie sleepily. "She's nose deep in that crazy book."

I opened the front door and almost stumbled over Aggie as she bounded out and jumped up in the swing with Cassie. I smiled fondly at the two of them as I turned to enter the house.

The front hall was dark after the sunshine outside and I bumped my knee painfully against an open drawer of the hall table that stood just inside the door.

"Damn!"

I closed the drawer with more force than necessary and limped my way through the house. Mother was curled up on her favorite chaise lounge on the back porch with Bethlehem Davis's manuscript on her lap—and a large magnifying glass in her hand—the one usually kept in the drawer of the table in the hall.

"You left the drawer open," I groused.

"Sorry, dear," she replied absently.

"Book good?"

"Umm."

I abandoned my mission to question Mother about Nell Jane Bradley's family history and went to the library to work on Leonard's own manuscript. This one was about international jewel thieves and diamond smugglers. I had just decided the book needed a wild ride or two through the crowded streets of Manhattan to spice it up. After this afternoon, I felt like I could do it justice; but just when I had Leonard on Forty-second Street in his souped up vintage Mustang, the Dairy Queen carbohydrates caught up with me. I stumbled over to one of the big red chintz-covered sofas in front of the fireplace, kicked off my shoes, and flopped down for a snooze.

"Very funny, Paisley. A little sophomoric, but amusing just the same. Now give me back the book."

"Ummph, wh...what?" I struggled up from the depths of a slightly erotic dream starring me and Pierce Brosnan to find my mother standing over me with stern, angry, disapproval written all over her face.

"The book, dear. Give me back the book," she demanded insistently. "It was just getting interesting."

"What book? I don't have any book. Beth's book?"

"Yes, of course, Beth's book. I dozed off for just a moment and when I opened my eyes it was gone. Cassie's sound asleep in the front porch swing with Aggie so it must have been you who took it. Give it back now, please."

I sat up, rubbed my eyes, and wiped the drool off my chin. Mother had both fists planted firmly on her trim waist and was actually tapping one foot impatiently on the Oriental rug. She looked mad and slightly ruffled—something that didn't happen often. I laughed.

"Paisley Sterling! What has gotten into you?" she snapped.

"I don't have Beth's book, Mother," I sighed, ending with a chuckle. "But whoever took it did me a favor. If it's really missing, I don't have to keep my promise to read it."

"Maybe, Cassie…," she began, a worried frown line only slightly creasing her smooth brow.

"Maybe, Cassie what?" asked my daughter from the doorway. She stretched her slim arms over her head and yawned, then crossed over to open the French doors so Aggie could take a run in the back yard. "What?" she repeated, as she turned and looked at us quizzically.

"Someone is playing a silly juvenile joke," observed Mother. "Only it's not very funny."

"Let me in on it," suggested Cassie. "I'll decide for myself if it's funny or not."

"Beth's book disappeared while Gran was asleep on the back porch."

"You think somebody broke into the house?"

Mother stared at her in amazement. "Well, maybe. I don't know. What do you think, Paisley?"

"Impossible!" interrupted my daughter. "Aggie didn't move a muscle. She would have barked if someone had tried to get in."

"Hah! The only thing that dog is good for is to make sure I keep my tetanus shots up to date."

"She only bit you three times, Mom!"

"Three times is right!" I retorted. "Just listen to yourself and imagine anyone else saying, 'my dog only bit my mom three times,' and see how stupid it sounds."

"Girls! Girls! Behave yourselves."

"We are not 'girls,' Gran. We are women," pontificated Cassie.

"Cassie's right, Mother. And you started this whole mess. I bet the manuscript pages slid off your lap while you were asleep. They're probably all in a heap under the chaise. You messed up the best dream I've had in months for nothing. It's not often that Pierce and I...."

"Who?" asked Mother with raised eyebrows.

"Never mind," I grumbled, as I stomped barefoot through the house, stubbing my toe painfully on a chair leg in the kitchen.

I got down on my hands and knees and peered under every table and chair on the back porch, but I didn't find even as much as a chewing gum wrapper.

"See!" demanded Mother righteously. "It's not here."

"You must have taken it inside and forgotten where you put it, Mother. Nobody came in here. The screen door is still hooked."

"She's right, Gran," said Cassie, as she crossed over to the door to let Aggie inside. "Hey, wait! Look at this! Somebody's slit the screen right at the edge of the door frame. The hole's just big enough to slip in a hand and unhook the door."

"And then take the time to hook it back?" I laughed. "Come on! What kind of joker would do a thing like that?"

"The kind who would think Miss Davis's book was worth stealing, I guess," answered Cassie.

"Yeah? What's up with that?" I chuckled, as I eased down into Mother's favorite chaise while she wasn't looking. I lay back in the cushions wondering if I could tempt Pierce into another dreamland rendezvous.

"Maybe the thief needed a doorstop," suggested Cassie, with a barely suppressed giggle.

"Or a...," I began.

"Stop it, you two," interrupted Mother. "You are being unkind—and quite without reason. Neither of you knows anything about the quality of Bethlehem's literary efforts."

"Okay, Mother. I'll buy into that," I allowed. "Just how

good was Beth's book?"

"Yes, Gran. What was it about?" asked Cassie, moving my feet aside to sit on the end of the chaise.

"I had not arrived at the, er, plot, just yet; but I think it could have been quite interesting. She had a few too many words in each sentence, perhaps...Paisley, that smirk is quite unattractive."

"Go on, Gran," urged Cassie.

"Well, the characters really held my attention, especially since some of them seemed very familiar."

I had closed my eyes, trying to conjure up a mental image of broad shoulders and a handsome, all-knowing smile; but something Mother said penetrated my daydream. "Familiar? How so?"

"I'm not positive, you understand, and I didn't get a chance to read very much; but I thought I recognized several people by her rather thinly veiled descriptions. And some of them, most of them as a matter-of-fact, were not very flattering portraits."

I sat up next to Cassie, all thoughts of dark, good-looking men forgotten. "You mean this was a 'tell all' book? My God! Maybe that's why it was flicked!" I jumped up and slapped my leg in excitement. Aggie raised her head from the cool flagstone floor and growled. "The sneaky little twit was probably privy to all sorts of juicy information she would never be allowed to publish in a small town newspaper –a newspaper whose income depends on advertisements from the local bigwigs she has the dirt on; but a racy novel about those same characters with fake names and a mustache or two.... Wow!"

"That's motive enough for someone to steal the book, all right," breathed Cassie.

"Yes, my girl!" I laughed. "Now I'm sorry I didn't take first dibs on the book myself. There are quite a few people in Rowan Springs I would like to see roasted slowly over the coals. I wonder if Beth has another copy."

"Perhaps you had better call on her and explain what has happened, Paisley. If she doesn't have a copy, she'll be quit distraught and will need a friendly shoulder to cry on."

"Oh, great! You lose the book and I become the bearer of ill tidings—and the owner of the damp shoulder. How come you can't go instead?"

"She needs a fellow writer—someone sympathetic who will understand her loss," explained Mother stiffly.

"Good grief!"

"Come on, Mom. Quit being a baby. I'll go with. After all, Miss Davis may not believe you, but I can back you up."

CHAPTER EIGHT

Where she acquired the knowledge I can't imagine, but Cassie knows where every single person in Rowan Springs lives. I drove while she gave me directions to a quiet cul-de-sac near the City County Park where Beth Davis resided. The shabby little brown cottage was set deep within a long, narrow lot filled with ancient water oaks and a jungle's worth of overgrown bamboo.

"Spooky," I observed, with a theatrical shudder.

"Mom, don't you dare!"

I stared at her with wide-eyed innocence. "What?"

"You know what! You're trying to scare me into leaving, so you can get out of fessing up to poor Miss Davis."

"I feel no qualms about telling Beth Davis what happened. I did absolutely nothing wrong. For once," I added under my breath.

Cassie had ears like a bat. "Okay, maybe you just don't want to have to explain why Gran was reading the book instead of you."

We got out of the car and walked slowly down the long winding path through the trees to the front door. On the way we passed a moss garden filled with plaster gnomes and painted mushrooms. A fake owl, eternally patient, sat on a bench watching the little people's endless frolic.

I shuddered—for real this time—and reluctantly followed Cassie up the walk. "I'm not kidding, Cassie," I whispered. "This place gives me the creeps! It's like Hansel and Gretel's worst nightmare."

She stopped until I caught up with her, then turned and shook her finger angrily in my face. "Mom, I told you not to do that!" she hissed. "You are not going to scare me into leaving!"

She grabbed my hand and pulled me the rest of the way to the front door.

"Knock!" she ordered, crossing her arms and staring sternly down at me.

"Why should I use my dainty knuckles when there is a perfectly good wrought-iron vampire bat...."

"That's a swallow, not a bat!"

I lifted the swallow/bat doorknocker and tapped loudly three times. "Nobody's home. Let's go." I turned and started walking away from the door.

Cassie reached out and grabbed my shirt tail. "Not so fast! Give her a chance to answer. She might be in the shower, or taking a nap, or...."

"Or asleep in a coffin in the basement?"

"I'm going to see if her car is in the garage."

"Cassie!"

But she had disappeared around the corner. I started to follow, then thought I heard a sound on the other side of the door. I placed my ear up against the wood and almost fell inside as it swung open into the gloom of a long hallway.

"Damn!" I stood still for a minute, listening. Somewhere water was dripping from a faucet, but that was the only sound I heard. "Beth?" I called tentatively, as I peered down the hallway into the darkness beyond. "Beth, it's Paisley Sterling. Are you home?"

An arm snaked out of the darkness and came to rest on my shoulder. I turned and screamed into Cassie's face. She jumped half a foot straight up, then screamed back at me.

"Mom! I told you not to do that! You scared me half to death!"

"And what about me, for God's sake! I'm an old lady! I could'a had a heart attack!"

"Yeah! Right!" She gave me a shove in the small of my back—propelling me down the dark hallway. "Get a move on. The car's in the garage. She must be in here somewhere."

"But...."

"But, nothing. I want to get this over with so we can go home. I could use a little normal right now, and I'm hungry. It's almost dinnertime." She paused and sniffed disdainfully. "Ugh! What's that smell?"

"Dusty rugs, sour mops, and old cooked cabbage."

"Miss Davis," she called out impatiently. "It's Cassie DeLeon. I'm here with my mom. Are you home?"

Cassie's voice echoed hollowly throughout the house. There was no answer.

"Let's go," I begged.

"Maybe she's in the back yard."

"Didn't you just go back there?"

"I went to the garage. The back yard's fenced in. I couldn't see over it. Come on."

"Cassie! Damn it!"

My intrepid daughter forged ahead and out of sight, leaving me alone again. It was getting dark outside, and even darker inside, but I had no choice. I crept down the hallway after Cassie. I was almost at the end when I heard her frightened call.

"Where are you?" I shouted back.

"Here! In the kitchen. Please hurry, Mommy. It's Miss Davis. She's had an accident. I think she may be dead."

I burst out of the hallway and into a dimly lit old-fashioned kitchen. My white-faced, terrified daughter was kneeling in the middle of the floor over the body of Bethlehem Davis.

"Is she dead?" I breathed.

"I...I don't think so," she answered. "I just saw her eyelids flicker."

"Well, don't just sit there—slap her, or something!"

Cassie sat back on her heels and looked at me indignantly. "You slap her!"

"Fine! I knelt down and raised my hand.

"Stop, Mom! I think she's coming around."

"Ummph!" moaned Beth Davis, dramatically—a little too dramatically, I thought. "Who am I?"

"Aren't they supposed to say, 'where am I'?" whispered Cassie.

"Yeah, I thought so, too," I told her.

"Miss Davis, what happened? Did you faint? Are you hurt? Should we call the ambulance? Do you have a doctor?"

"For Pete's sake, Cassie! Give the poor thing a chance."

The "poor thing" fluttered her scant eyelashes rapidly, and tried to sit up. I placed a hand on her shoulder and held her down. "Not so fast, Beth. Let's be a trifle cautious here until we know what happened."

"What did happen, Miss Davis?" repeated Cassie.

"Someone hit me on the head. I...I can't remember anymore."

Against her feeble protests I felt around under Beth's hair, but I failed to discover any bumps, or soggy, mushy places that I supposed might represent a fractured skull.

"Everything seems okay, but I really think you should have someone check you out. If you don't have a personal physician...."

"I don't want a doctor!"

"Mom's right, Miss Davis. And her doctor is just great."

"How many times do I have to repeat myself? I can't really remember a bitching thing, but I'm sure from looking around at this filthy dump that I'm not rolling in dough. No quacks! And no cops! Now move you arses and help me up!"

Cassie and I looked at each other in complete surprise. I spoke first. "Okay, who are you, and what have you done with Beth Davis?"

"That's what I've been trying to get across to youse dames. I don't know nothin' about this Davis broad, and I don't remember who the hell I am. What's it to ya? Now, help me up off this stinking, lousy floor, or beat it."

Cassie and I pulled the woman formerly known as Bethlehem Davis up off the floor so fast she almost fell forward. She brushed off her yellow skirt and turned to face us. "Got any booze in this fleabag?"

"I'm calling the ambulance," declared Cassie. "This is just way too bizarre."

I agreed wholeheartedly with my daughter, so we held Beth's kicking and screaming body until the Rowan Springs EMS team arrived to take her off our hands. One injection of their magic juice in her derriere, and Beth Davis—or whoever she was—no longer presented a problem.

"We can't knock her out completely because she hit her head," explained the ambulance driver. "That injection was just to calm her down. Can't have 'em runnin' amuck on the way to the hospital. Who's her MD?"

"I don't know if she has one," I told him. "Call Dr. Dhanvantari on your radio, if you don't mind. Tell him Paisley Sterling needs a favor, and ask him to meet you at the hospital."

"Sure thing," he shouted, as he backed rapidly out of the driveway.

"Let's snoop around a bit," I suggested to Cassie with a wink and a leer.

"Mom!"

"I know, I know. It's totally un-kosher; but we may not get another chance, and I'd like to see how our little friend—whoever she may be—lives. Besides, even though I think she must have been mistaken, she did say someone hit her over the head. We owe it to her to see if there are any signs of a break-in."

"I don't know, Mom," worried my proper daughter. "What if one of the neighbors comes over to find out what happened?"

"We can say we getting some of her things together to take to the hospital. As a matter of fact, that's a great idea! You look in her bedroom for some gowns and slippers and stuff like that, and I'll look around the rest of the house for her toothbrush."

"Mom!"

"And hurry!"

Darkness had gobbled up the interior of the house, but I could still see some daylight through the wide slats of the old-fashioned Venetian blinds in the parlor. I pulled the musty draperies shut before I turned on the lights so I wouldn't be observed from the outside.

The room had a depressingly faded look. Colors that had once been bright and vibrant had turned to sad and sorry beiges, and dark dingy maroons. The rug, the overstuffed chair and sofa, and the ancient ottoman looked as if they were cut from the same mangy old cloth.

Everywhere dust could gather it had done so, and with a vengeance. The soft, gray veneer of years of indifferent housekeeping covered every surface to further rob the room of color and life. I could tell with one glance that nothing in here had been disturbed for months. I moved on.

The kitchen was cleaner, but still had the same forlorn air of disuse. I checked the back door, just in case, but found no signs of forced entry. Of course, I had practically fallen in the front door, so that proved nothing.

The freezer was empty except for a half-eaten ice cream cake with a garish picture of Barbie and the salutation, "Happy Birthday Zel...." Ten little plastic containers of coleslaw from the Dairy Queen sat alone on a shelf in the refrigerator below.

The knotty pine kitchen cabinets had that sticky feel of old grease which accumulates after years of frying food on an unvented stovetop. I gingerly opened each cabinet door, but found only a few cans of tuna and some moldering roach tablets.

"Any luck?" asked Cassie from the doorway.

"Nope. And I'm bored. Let's go. This house is making me depressed."

"Maybe you'd like to see what I found."

"What?" I asked, my interest perking up.

"Follow me, my pretty," she cackled in her best crone's voice.

Beth Davis had apparently spent all of her decorating energy and a great deal of money on her bedroom. The place fairly glowed and shimmered with rich velvets and lush satins. Spindly, imitation French Provençal night tables decorated with hand-painted cherubs stood on each side of a large canopied bed. Purple satin curtains with golden tassels hung from the canopy frame, partially hiding the heavy crimson velvet bedspread and the multitude of satin throw pillows scattered in an air of calculated abandon.

"My God! It looks like a bordello!"

Cassie laughed. "How many bordellos have you been in, Mom?"

I shook my head and grinned. "Well, it looks like one of Leonard Paisley's favorite bordellos, anyway."

"And guess what I found," she said proudly, as she pulled back one of the heavy velvet panels behind the bed and pointed to a shiny, new stainless steel wall safe. "Wonder what's in there," she said, pointedly. "Does Leonard know how to open a safe?"

"Sure, but I don't—at least not without the key, or combination, or whatever."

"Key—in this case," she said. "That's kind of old-fashioned, isn't it?"

I got close enough to examine the mirror surface of the safe more carefully. The slightly distorted reflection of my face stared back at me against the opulent background of red velvet and purple satin, but there was not even a fingerprint to mar the finish. "She must polish this damn thing every day!"

"The whole room is like that," Cassie told me. "Spic and span—not a spot of dust or dirt anywhere."

"Did you look under the bed?"

Her eyes and her mouth opened wide in speculation as she dropped to her knees by the side of the bed. I raced around to the other side and was there to meet her gaze as we stared at each other from beneath the fringe of the bedspread.

"See anything?" she asked.

"Not even a dust bunny," I admitted.

The thick plush carpet felt good under my elbows, and I relaxed for a moment. "I'm tired, and hungry, Cassie. You were right the first time. Let's go home."

"Party pooper! It's just getting interesting."

"So is.... Hey, what's that?"

Cassie had gotten up, but she quickly lay back down and pulled up her side of the heavy bedspread. "What?" she asked, poking her head under the bed frame.

"That little black plastic thingie tucked up under the bed rail right above your head. If you reach up and stretch as far as you can over to the right you can get it. There! What is it?"

Cassie grunted with the effort of bending like a pretzel, then crawled out from under the bed. "Looks like one of those little audio cassettes."

"Take it," I said.

"Mom! That's stealing!"

"Then give it to me, and I'll take it."

"That would make me an accessory," she protested.

"Okay! Then leave it on the table so I can 'find it' and take it."

"Oh, for Pete's sake!" She stuck the cassette in her jeans pocket. "There! Happy?"

CHAPTER NINE

When we heard a tentative knocking at the front door we knew Cassie's prediction had come true: one of Beth's curious neighbors had come to inquire about her. Fortunately, Cassie had already gathered our invalid's clothes in an overnight bag so it was easy to explain why we were still here.

"I do hope dear little Beth is going to be all right," moaned Maggie Lyons through a forest of crooked, tobacco-stained teeth. "She's such a pleasant neighbor. Such a quiet little thing. I hardly know when she's home."

"I'm sure she'll be fine, ma'am," said Cassie, reassuringly.

"How's that?" shouted the old woman. "You'll have to speak up. Young people don't have any manners these days. Just mumble, they do."

As we followed Maggie Lyons outside and locked the door behind us, I noticed that the old woman practically got whiplash trying to see the interior of the house. Maggie Lyons might be a neighbor, but I had a feeling there hadn't been many chatty invitations to share a cup of Beth's coffee. Maggie didn't know how lucky she was. I wouldn't want a cup of anything from that kitchen.

When Cassie offered to drive to the hospital, I didn't argue. I wanted to poke through the overnight bag to see what she had brought for Beth.

"Feathers?"

"I couldn't find anything without them, or something equally as ridiculous. Believe it or not, that little number was the most conservative nightgown she had."

"You've got to be kidding?" I held up the filmy fuchsia nylon, then paused to blow a bit of errant ostrich plume off the end of my nose. "Wow! A feather bosom—and this was the

51

most conservative gown?"

"At least that one has a bosom."

"Oh."

We found our patient was sleeping peacefully in Room 241 when we got to the Lakeland County Hospital. Cassie busied herself by putting Beth's scanties away while I went to find the doctor.

Saijad Dhanvantari was just winding up the dictation of a surgical procedure on another patient when I spotted him.

"Ah, Paisley, little sister," he said with a warm welcoming smile. "How very pleasant to see you."

"How's it going, Saijad? Married life agreeing with you?"

Indira Dhanvantari was not as fond of me as was her husband—even though I had been the catalyst that had put the ring on her finger. After having me as a patient, she had threatened to return to Calcutta and become one of Mother Theresa's nuns—until Saijad promised to marry her instead.

"Ah! My life is full of charm and beauty," he said with a wry grin. "My lovely wife has made me happier than I have ever been before. I know because Indira herself reminds me of this very thing several times a day."

"Goodness, Saijad!" I laughed. "I'm really sorry I had to pull you away from so much wedded bliss."

"Do not be sorry, little sister. My beloved bride is a strict vegetarian, and the one thing I find myself missing above all others is a double bacon cheeseburger. This unexpected medical emergency will allow me to satisfy my fondest desire before I return to my happy home." He looked up at me and solemnly winked one handsome dark-brown eye. "Do you, perhaps, have a Tic-Tac on your person? I wish to enjoy this double bacon cheeseburger with onions and pickles."

Saijad carefully tucked away the lint-covered breath mint Cassie fished out of her pocket before he checked his patient's chart one last time.

"Miss Bethlehem Davis is very okay, I think. I found nothing untoward in her physical examination, and the radiological series of her skull was negative."

"Then how come she acted so strangely when she woke up?" I insisted.

"Ah!"

My learned physician would say no more except that he would return to check on his patient in the morning.

"What's his hurry?" asked Cassie.

"It's a marital thing," I answered cryptically.

Cassie and I sat by Beth's hospital bed and listened to her snore for a full ten minutes before I complained. "This is stupid!"

"It's the right thing to do," explained Cassie patiently.

"What? Sit here all night—bored to death?"

"We're just being kind and neighborly."

"Well, I've never been accused of being kind, and I'm definitely not Beth's neighbor. Let one of those plaster gnomes, or that old witch who lives next door sit here and watch her breathe for the next eight hours. I'm going home."

Cassie's sigh was deep and heavy with unspoken criticism as she got up to leave with me.

"Okay! So I'm not only being unkind, I'm a first-class pig with no redeeming social value whatsoever."

"You said it, Mom."

"Double bacon cheeseburger?"

"Good heavens! Isn't one flirtation a week with death enough for you?"

I followed her out of the room and down the hall as she spouted dire nutritional warnings and predictions of my early demise. I let her pontificate on my total lack of character and self-control until we were back in Watson and pulling out of the hospital parking lot.

"So! All said and done—double bacon cheeseburger?"

"Sure. Why not," she grumbled. "Life won't be nearly as much fun without you. I might as well go along for the ride."

"Hooray! Let's get takeout—and something for Gran and Aggie, too. We can eat on the back porch by candlelight. And by the way, Tootsie, that was one of the sweetest things you've ever said to me."

"Good grief!"

Mother left a note saying that she was at the Country Club with Horatio, and Cassie refused to allow me seconds, so Aggie had an abundant surprise in her doggie bowl. She gobbled down everything but the pickles.

I gazed longingly at the empty dog dish. "I would have

loved those pickles. Maybe I could wash them off and...."

"Mom! You're impossible!" declared my concerned daughter. "That's it! I'm putting you on a sprout and Tofu diet tomorrow."

"Then we might as well go back for a hot fudge sundae while we can," I retorted with what I considered to be my most winning smile.

Cassie through up her hands in disgust and stormed off to her room with Aggie trotting behind her—well, maybe not trotting, waddling is more like it.

I waddled off to the Dairy Queen all by myself, but I never got my sundae. On impulse, I decided to check out the Davis's homestead by moonlight when one of Watson's tires went flat and I discovered that I had no spare.

I sat on the curb hoping that someone would come along, but after about fifteen fruitless minutes I gave up. Ten o'clock was late for folks who were early to rise, and most people in this quiet, working class neighborhood had gone to bed.

I left Watson sitting forlornly by the curbside and struck off on foot in the direction of Beth's house. Maggie Lyons had the look of a night owl to me. I hoped that if she were still up watching the evening news, or maybe an old movie, she wouldn't mind letting me inside to use the phone. I forgot about her being partially deaf.

I banged on the front door until my hands ached, then finally gave up trying to make the old hag hear me and decided to try and get her attention another way. I squeezed through the prickly hedges underneath the high front windows, but I was too short to reach the sill.

"Damn!" I swore softly.

The hedge pulled at my hair and tore my shirt as I backed out into the yard. I was trying to brush off any hitch-hiking creepy crawlers when I tripped and fell over the lawn sprinkler and wound up sitting in a big, squishy mud puddle. I pounded the wet grass with my fists and heels, venting my mounting frustration by cursing loudly and energetically in Spanish.

I was cold—cold and wet up to my earlobes. The night wasn't getting any younger and I needed a telephone. Beth Davis had one in her ugly little kitchen. I decided to get to that phone if I had to break the door down.

It took me three tries before I managed to slip and slide to my feet. My moccasins were full of water and my jeans were soaked and caked with mud by the time I stood precariously upright. I kicked off my shoes in disgust and slogged through the muddy yard to the gravel drive in my bare feet. Hopping and cursing as the sharp little rocks bit into my tender insteps, I danced across the driveway into Beth's yard like a spastic marionette.

Two gnomes and a concrete mushroom were in the path I chose to lead me to the back of the cottage. Quite predictably, I managed to stub my toes painfully on both gnomes and fall over the mushroom.

I lay on the wet grass trying to control my temper when I heard a police siren howling around the corners of the quiet neighborhood. With enormous effort, I struggled to my feet and ran clumsily toward the shadowy protection of Beth's house.

I raced around to the back—stumbling over empty clay flowerpots and making so much noise that the intruder already inside the house heard me. I only got a glimpse through the kitchen window, but the dark-hooded figure with the burning eyes filled me with primitive, spine-tingling terror. Then *whatever-it-was* grabbed a skillet off the stove and used it to smash the ceiling light.

I stopped dead in my tracks—paralyzed with fear—waiting helplessly for the creature to fly out of the kitchen window and attack me. It was a huge relief to hear the sounds of pounding footsteps behind me and a deep voice shouting, "You, there! Hands up! And no funny business!"

CHAPTER TEN

I surrendered eagerly to one of Rowan Springs's finest by throwing myself into his beefy arms and screaming, "Save me! The monster!"

"It's okay, lady! Calm down, now. I don't want to have to give you a taste of this little old cattle.... Oops!"

The shock from the Taser sent me thudding to the ground where I lay speechless—unable to move even the smallest muscle. The big cop dragged my muddy, barefoot carcass to his cruiser and propped me against the back door while he retrieved a sheet of blue plastic from the trunk. With practiced ease, he wrapped the sheet around my filthy body, dumped me in the back seat, and slammed the car door shut.

I tried my best to move, but the powerful electric current had left me paralyzed. We were half way to the county jail before I could summon up the strength to spit the mud and dirt out of my mouth. I coughed and tried to swallow, but my tongue felt as thick as a medium-sized boa constrictor.

When the cop opened the door and dragged me out of the car, all I could do was croak Andy Joiner's name. "Aaannthy! Aaannthy Jahhhnn!"

"I know, lady," the big cop said soothingly. "Them D.T.'s is the worst. But just settle down, please. I'd really hate to zap a little bit of a thing like you again."

I shut my mouth obediently as he hefted me easily over his broad shoulders and carried me to the one and only cell in the Rowan County Jail reserved for female miscreants. Unfortunately, it was in the back—far away from all the others—and Andy's office. When the officer dropped my unresisting body on the hard bottom bunk, I knew I was there for the night. Trying to get Andy's attention would probably get me nothing more than another session with the Taser, so I closed my eyes and let my abused and exhausted mind and body slip into an uneasy darkness.

When I opened my eyes again, Andy was watching me from a chair on the opposite side of the cell. I tried to sit up, but the cocoon of blue plastic sheeting held me prisoner.

"Do you mind?" I groaned. "I have to pee in the worst way."

If I hadn't been so uncomfortable on just about every level, I would have laughed at Andy's red-faced embarrassment as he jumped up and fumbled for his pocketknife.

"Careful!" I ordered, as he slit the plastic away from my body and helped me up. I staggered and grabbed onto his shoulder for a moment until the dizziness passed.

"You okay?"

"Well, let me see," I answered, my voice heavy with sarcasm. "My clothes are ruined. My favorite shoes are missing. I'm a filthy, muddy mess—and a criminal to boot."

Andy gave me a big, slow grin. "Forget the criminal bit, Paisley. I got Mrs. Lyons calmed down as soon as I found out that you were the bull in her china shop. And Billy Martin admits that he didn't smell any alcohol on your breath."

"Billy Martin?"

"The officer who arrested you."

"Then why in the hell did he arrest me?" I demanded hotly. "I wasn't doing anything wrong!"

Andy blushed again. "He said you were acting weird."

I felt the anger subside. Billy Martin was right, but I wasn't sure I wanted to tell Andy why I was acting weird, or what I had seen in Beth Davis's kitchen last night—at least not just yet.

"Can you give me some privacy?" I asked instead.

"I can do better than that. The female employees of the county EMS have a shower in back of the fire station next door. I have some fresh overalls if you want to clean up before you go home."

"Yes! By the way, I hope you let my family know that I'm not dead in a ditch somewhere."

Andy grinned. "Called Cassie last night and again this morning to tell her when to pick you up. You'll just have time for that shower, if you hurry."

I grabbed the orange cotton overalls Andy proffered and headed for the shower. Twenty minutes later I was drinking my second cup of tea in his office, and trying not to lose my cool while he and Cassie had a big laugh over my predicament.

"No wonder Mr. Martin thought you were drunk, Mom!"

"Yeah, yeah, can we go home now?"

Cassie was having a grand old time at my expense. Her brown eyes sparkled with mischief and her cheeks were rosy and flushed from laughter. I had a hard time staying mad at her.

"And it was so sweet of him to go back to Mrs. Lyon's yard and dig your shoes out of that mud puddle."

"He's a peach, all right. Now can we go?"

"Take her home, Cassie," ordered Andy. "Feed her some breakfast and let her get some real sleep. I keep a clean jail, but nobody could accuse me of having the most comfortable beds in town."

"You can say that again!" I groused. "And don't worry! I'll send this little orange polyester-cotton number back as soon as I can."

Unfortunately, Cassie had parked Mother's baby blue Lincoln right smack dab in front of the jail. For a moment I considered asking her to move the car to the back so I could get in without being seen, but I figured it was already too late. Everybody in town had probably known before they ate breakfast that Anna Howard Sterling's daughter spent the night as an unwilling guest of the Lakeland County taxpayers.

"What are you doing, Mom?" demanded Cassie, as I sauntered insolently around the front of the car for the second time.

"Waving," I answered with a big wicked smile. "Waving—just in case somebody hasn't seen me yet."

"Get in," she ordered. "Officer Martin was right. You are acting weird."

I climbed in the car and leaned back in the soft leather seat with a satisfied sigh. "Take me home, Jeeves, and if you don't mind, stop at the Dairy Que...."

"No!" interrupted my outraged daughter. "No more fat and sugar for you! I'm convinced that if you eat more sensibly, you'll behave more sensibly."

"Wow, that's quite a leap!"

"I'm worried about you, Mom," she sighed. "You're not getting any younger...."

"Oh, stop! If I promise to cut out the cheeseburgers and fries, will you cut out the sermonizing? And please, no more references to the grim reaper." I shuddered, suddenly remembering the dark-hooded figure I had seen last night.

"Are you cold?" Cassie asked with quick concern. "I'm sorry, Mom. You've had a terrible experience, and I've been making fun of you. I'll get you home as soon as possible, then tuck you in and bring you breakfast in bed. How does that sound?"

"Fine, as long as there are no sprouts involved."

Cassie was true to her word. She tucked me up in my big four-poster bed and brought me a sensible breakfast of poached eggs, toast and tea, all of which I devoured in about three minutes flat.

"That was very satisfying, Cassie. Thanks very much," I sighed. "But if you don't mind, I'll save the plain, non-fat, aspartame-sweetened yogurt and wheat berries for later."

Cassie didn't blink an eye. She removed the tray to my dressing table and returned to the bed to sit at my feet. "Okay, Mom. 'Fess up. What really happened last night?"

"I might have known there was a price tag on all this tender loving care," I grumbled.

"Mom! That's mean!" she cried, jumping up to leave.

"Oh, Cassie, please don't go! I'm just kidding. Besides, I know Mother is probably going to chew me out about last night and I really need an ally."

She grudgingly returned to sit beside me. "You're right about Gran," she said. "She was pretty ticked off when Andy called and woke her up to say you were in the poky. Apparently, you're the first Sterling to have that dubious distinction."

"Oh, God! It's going to be worse than I thought," I moaned. "Mother will never forgive me."

"I'm afraid you're right," she agreed. "So you might as well distract yourself by telling me what you were doing at Beth's house last night. She's all right, by the way."

"Who?"

"Beth Davis, of course. I called the hospital this morning before I came to pick you up."

My pillows felt wonderful as I scooted down in the soft welcoming comfort of the silken sheets. "It's all her fault," I decided, morosely. "If she hadn't fainted and knocked her head on the kitchen floor...."

Cassie braced her back against one of the four posters before she dropped the bomb. "Dr. Dhanvantari thinks someone really did hit Beth from behind."

"You're kidding!" I said, sitting up straight in bed. "With the infamous blunt object, I suppose?"

"Something like that. At any rate, Beth didn't just faint away. Someone knocked her down before we got to her—just like she said."

Cassie leaned up closer to me and whispered, "Do you think that 'someone' was still in the house while we were there?" She shivered theatrically. "Could we have been in mortal danger?"

"I suppose so, but I just can't believe...."

"Well, Dr. D. does. He spouted some medical jargon that means Beth's eyes look funny, which—and I quote, 'is the result of a forceful blow to the occiput'."

"Cassie, do you remember anything strange about Beth's house?"

She laughed, and stretched like a cat across the bottom of the bed. "Sure," she answered with a yawn. "It was a moldy, dusty, mildewy mess except for that wild and wicked bedroom."

"No, that's not all," I said, shaking my head, as if the movement would invigorate my brain and help me to remember more. "I heard water dripping when I first entered the house, but I forgot about it when you came back around from the garage and scared me half to death. Do you remember if the kitchen sink was wet?"

"What are you getting at, Mom? You think maybe there's a homicidal plumber on the loose?"

Cassie's yawn was contagious, and the long, exhausting night was finally catching up with me. "I don't know why it seems so important," I said with a shrug. "Maybe if I get some shuteye first...."

CHAPTER ELEVEN

When I woke up, I discovered that Mother was really, really mad—even madder than she had been when I staged a fake protest at the Atlanta Park Zoo because they had no Pandas. That little incident got my face plastered on newspapers from coast to coast, but I was just a student then, and immaturity was my excuse for inappropriate behavior. That wouldn't work now. Mother firmly believed that once you attained the age of thirty, mistakes in judgment were no longer acceptable. And then there were other considerations.

"Have you forgotten that you are a Sterling?" she inquired, in that cool, calm way she has when harboring an explosive volcano within.

"No, Mother," I answered, my head respectfully bowed.

"Our family has certain standards which we must uphold as an example to rest of the community."

"Yes, Mother."

"Were you inebriated, Paisley?"

"Oh, for Pete's sake!" I exclaimed, stepping neatly into her well-laid trap. "You know I never drink enough to do anything that stupid!"

Her smile was warm and lovely, and very lethal. "Then, perhaps, you have some other excuse for your stupidity, dear?" She paused in front of the hall mirror to smooth the collar of her smart beige silk suit before she zoomed in for the kill. "Horatio is taking me to the Country Club for luncheon so I can initiate damage control. Perhaps together we can quell the tide of your impending notoriety. Maybe I should volunteer to head their next charity bazaar. What do you think, Cassandra, dear?" she asked, turning to her granddaughter. "It's for a very good cause—the Rowan Springs Home for the Impetuous and Foolhardy. You may have to commit your mother to their care someday."

Furious that my bare feet made no satisfying sound when I stomped back to my bedroom, I released my mounting frustration by childishly slamming the door. It served no purpose, however, because I could hear the silvery peal of Mother's laughter even through the feathers of the pillow I held over my head.

"Damn! Damn, and rats!"

I spit out a mouthful of dog hair and threw the offending pillow/doggie bed across the room just as my daughter opened the door. Instead of catching the pillow, she stepped neatly aside and watched open-mouthed as it landed with a crash on top of my dresser.

"Wow!" she exclaimed, as the last bottle of perfume skidded across the floor and smashed into the opposite wall. "That's some smell! Do you want me to call 'the home' and reserve your room, or should I get some paper towels and help you clean up?"

"Oh, Cassie! I've made such a terrible mess of things," I moaned, as I sank down on my bed.

"Don't be so hard on yourself, Mom. Last night was kind of a screw up, I have to admit—but it worked out okay. And Gran just left, so we have plenty of time to clean this up before she gets back. Besides," she said, picking up broken pieces of fancy little bottles. "You hate this stuff. I don't know why you ever kept it in the first place."

"Birthday presents," I sniffed. "And Christmas...."

"You never even wear scent," she rambled on, ignoring me, "except for that Cartier that Daddy gave you. And while we're on the subject, Mom, after twenty-something years, it's getting a bit stale."

That was the last straw. I threw myself down on the bed and sobbed with abandon—even ignoring my stricken daughter when she came to sit beside me.

"Oh, Mom, I'm so sorry! I'll get you some more perfume, I promise. What would you like? Gucci, Pucci, or sushi?"

I stopped crying to laugh at her silly joke and discovered that I was all cried out. "Never mind, Cassie," I sniffed. "You're right. The Cartier is a bit off, and I did hate all those other perfumes. I just kept them because the bottles were pretty."

"You kept them because you were afraid Gran would get mad if you threw away her expensive gifts."

"Right, as usual," I sighed, giving her a hug.

"You're too old to worry about what your mother thinks," she decided.

"I don't know," I argued, crossing over into the bathroom to wash my face at the sink. "Do you ever really get too old to care about a mother's opinion?" I walked out of the bathroom swabbing my face with a cool washcloth. "Cassie?"

My daughter pointedly ignored me as she searched for more bits of broken glass. "I think we'll need the vacuum for this job," she declared. "I'll go get it."

I never did get an answer to my question because we jumped headfirst into another mess when we used Mother's expensive new vacuum cleaner to suck up the glass.

"Well," said Cassie, delicately holding her nose. "We'll just change the bag. That'll take away the smell, won't it?"

It didn't. Neither did washing down the innards of the fancy Hoover with rubbing alcohol, or spraying them with Lysol."

"Oh, my God," I moaned. "What next?"

"The phone," said Cass. "I'll get it."

I held my head in my hands and prayed that nothing else had gone wrong, but it just wasn't my day.

"Mom. It's Dr. D. from the hospital. Beth's gone missing."

Saijad was very sorry to have to tell me, but sometime during the morning—sometime after the seven o'clock nursing shift checked on her—Bethlehem Davis disappeared from her hospital room.

"But how can that be?" I asked him, frustration creeping into my voice. "She was under your personal care!"

"Ah, little sister," he explained. "You must forgive me, but I am not a jailer to keep my patients under lock and key."

"Is that a dig?" I demanded angrily. But Saijad was totally incapable of sarcasm. He was, however, not above dissolving into fits of laughter when I filled him in on my little escapade of the night before.

I hung up on him.

I felt terrible. My two hour nap had done very little towards alleviate the nagging backache caused by eight hours of restless sleep on a hard bunk, and now my sinuses were rebelling fiercely against competing fragrances—attar of roses, violet, bergamot, gardenia, and orange blossoms. Nevertheless, I knew what we had to do.

"We have to find her, Cassie," I managed to blurt out between sneezes.

"For heaven's sake, why? She's not our problem!"

"Isn't she?" I sniffed. "Think about it, Cassie. None of this would have happened if she hadn't given me her manuscript."

"Whoa! That's quite a stretch even for you," she admitted "What makes you think even for a moment that Beth's manuscript has anything to do with it?"

Instead of answering, I rummaged through the refrigerator, finally taking out some Gouda and country ham butter. "Cassie, do we have any of those little Bremner wafers left? They go so well with cheese."

She was sitting on the kitchen floor trying to reassemble the smelly vacuum cleaner. "In the pantry," she answered absentmindedly—intent on her task.

I managed to gobble down three cracker sandwiches before she noticed what I was eating and took it away from me.

"I suppose you're right about our trying to find Beth," she sighed, as she measured out a minuscule dot of low-fat blue cheese dressing on top of my spinach and arugula salad." But where do we start? We certainly can't set foot near her house again."

"Can't we?"

"Mom! You haven't learned a thing from all this!"

"See! I told you nutrition had nothing to do with it! 'Impetuous and foolhardy' is my middle name. It doesn't matter what I eat! Pass the Gouda, please."

My favorite wardrobe items were in the laundry room in a brown paper bag labeled, "Evidence—Rowan Springs Jail." They would have to undergo some big time cleaning before I could wear them again. I only hoped that my Cole-Haan moccasins could be salvaged. They were the second pair I had gone through this year.

I finally settled on a pair of old chinos, soft and frayed

from years of wear, and a pale blue cotton polo. Shoes were a bigger problem, however. My feet were spoiled—soft and tender from three years of nothing but sock feet, bare feet, and moccasins. Leather loafers were not an option, even though I had enjoyed wearing them once upon a time—and the thick dimpled soles of tennis shoes tripped me up and made me clumsy.

I sneezed again—this time because of dust in the back of my closet—and wiped my nose on a piece of tissue paper from a shoebox. I was still tired, my head was stuffy, and my neck was getting stiff; but I just couldn't sit here like a bump on a pickle. No matter what Cassie had said, I knew there was something sinister going on, and I was determined to find out what it was.

I held my arms above my head and stretched, wincing more at the ominous popping sound of protesting tendons than at the pain. I looked at the ceiling while I counted slowly to ten, then stretched some more. My neck felt better, but as I stared upwards my mind was instantly flooded with pictures of Beth's little cottage and I knew we had to get there before it was too late.

CHAPTER TWELVE

"Bedroom slippers, Mom!" protested Cassie. "Don't you think that's a little eccentric even for you? What if someone sees us?"

"They won't," I muttered, as I drove slightly above Horatio's speed towards Beth's dreary little abode.

"And what's the big hurry?" continued Cassie. "So what, if she has an attic. Everybody has an attic in Rowan Springs. Well...except maybe for those new fake European stucco monstrosities out on Country Club Drive, and even they have crawl spaces."

"I bet we'll find that Beth Davis has a lot more than a crawl space!"

Cassie braced herself against dashboard as I negotiated a particularly dicey turn. When I swerved coming out of it because one of my shaggy purple bedroom shoes caught on the gas pedal she gasped in alarm. "Where's the fire, Mom!"

"Here, apparently," I told her as we pulled up to the curb. "And we're too late," I announced, my voice full of grim disappointment

Thick, dark, smoke—fed by the flames feasting hungrily on the house below—billowed from the charred roof of the Davis cottage. The fire truck had arrived long before we got there, but the firemen were simply going through the motions. It was obvious that nothing they could do would make any difference.

It was not my house, but just the same, I was almost moved to tears. Poor little house, I thought, sadly. With a little tender loving care: a new coat of paint—some shutters here, a porch there—it might have been attractive. Instead it was dying as it had lived—ugly and unkempt—and I was fairly positive—

taking some pretty big secrets to the grave.

"Damn!"

Cassie had gotten out of the car and perched herself on the hood. She was quiet—watching intently as the hot, sweaty men drained the fire hoses and coiled them back on the truck. I got out and joined her.

The wind—the one that had helped to fan the fire—now assisted in carrying the smoke up and away—across the trees and beyond, gradually clearing the air so that only the pungent smell of wet ashes remained.

"You think Beth was in the attic, don't you, Mom?"

I heard the catch in her voice, and turned quickly to see tears streaking down her smooth cheeks.

"No!" I exclaimed, putting my arms around her. "That's not what I think at all!" But as the words slipped past my lips, I began to doubt them. I bit my own lip to keep from saying anything to alarm Cassie, but I suddenly realized that she might be right.

In my desire to comfort my daughter, I didn't notice Andy Joiner until he was practically under my nose. "What's going on, Paisley?" he asked, suspiciously. "You all mourning a house? That's kinda queer, don't you think?" He looked down and laughed. "What's with the hairy purple feet? You look like a Muppet."

"Andy, was...did you find...anything, anyone...?" I stammered

"Why no," he answered, looking perplexed. "The house was vacant. Miss Davis lived alone, and she's in the hospital."

"No, she's not," I told him, urgently. "Saijad Dhanvantari called about an hour ago. Beth disappeared from the hospital some time this morning."

"Excuse me," he said brusquely, his smile vanishing into a grim, tight line. He hurried back over toward the tired firemen who were huddled around the rear end of the fire truck. The men were relaxing—drinking from a big water cooler and enjoying a hamper of sandwiches. Andy had them mobilized in less than a minute. Tuna fish, pimento cheese, and paper cups were trampled underfoot as the firemen hurriedly pulled their heavy jackets back over sweaty arms and wet undershirts. They grabbed their axes and ran back to the smoldering ruins of the house, thrusting aside smoking beams and kicking away fallen timbers—heedless of their own safety.

The exhausted men searched for over an hour, but found nothing. When they finally piled back on the fire truck and pulled out of the driveway past us I turned away—embarrassed that I had caused so much trouble.

"Never mind, Mom," chirped Cassie, happily. "Thank God that Beth wasn't in there, but you could have been right!" She shivered at the thought, completely overlooking the fact that it was she who had started unrolling this particular ball of yarn. "I'll help Gran make some cookies next week. We can take them a bunch. You always love going to the station to see the fire truck."

"Not any more," I mumbled glumly.

I looked up to see Andy lumbering towards us. He was covered in soot from head to toe, and his uniform was ruined: one sleeve was completely torn away and his trouser cuffs were charred and smoking. It was obvious that he was not very happy with me.

"The fellows said to thank you for that little exercise in futility, Paisley," he grumbled.

"Really? Those were their exact words?"

"Of course not! I'm too much of a gentleman to tell you what they really said, but maybe someday if you push me...."

"Okay, okay! I get the drift. I'm sorry, Andy. But if she had been in there...?"

He wiped his face with the back of his hand, smearing soot and sweat across his mouth, and started to say something—instead, he did the oddest thing. Andy Joiner licked the back of his hand and smacked his lips as if savoring the finest wine. "That's strange," he said. "I wouldn't have ever suspected a fire like this...." He caught himself before finishing his sentence, and turned quickly on his heels to head for his car.

"What's going on, Andy?" I called after him. "What's strange?" I yelled, as he backed rapidly out to the street without even a glance at me. "I could sue you for false arrest, you know! You'd better tell me!"

Cassie pulled me gently towards Mother's car and stuffed me inside. Maggie Lyons was standing in her doorway watching us—sour disapproval written all over her wrinkled old face.

"I could sue you, too—you old witch!" I hollered in Spanish at the top of my voice.

She shook a gnarled fist in the air, and shouted back, "Damn foreigners! Go back where you come from!" She slammed her front door, then opened it again to hurl one more insult. "And learn how to dress like decent folk!"

Cassie was laughing so hard she had to pull into the First Fidelity parking lot to keep from wrecking the Lincoln. "Oh, Mom!" she gasped. "Don't you see? Maggie Lyons is Gran's alter ego! They must have been separated at birth."

While I didn't fail to see the humor of the situation, I was too busy mulling over Andy's behavior to join in the fun. It made my daughter mad.

"Well, it was funny!" Cassie pouted, as she turned back into Main Street and headed for home.

"Sorry, honey," I apologized. "You'll have to forgive me—too little sleep, and too many questions." I stretched back in the comfort of the leather seat and propped my purple feet on the dashboard. "What do you suppose Andy tasted in that soot?" I wondered out loud.

"Oh, great! Now I suppose you'll want to go back there and eat ashes! Won't Maggie Lyons just love that! And don't count on Andy to be so forgiving this time around. Not to mention the fact that Gran will probably disown you, and I'll have to sneak out of the house to visit you in the penitentiary."

"Amazing, isn't it?" I asked no one in particular. "Everyone in my family is certain I'm going to end up in some sort of institution."

"Why did we race over to Beth's house in the first place, Mom? You promised to tell me."

"Beth had to live somewhere," I explained. "That fancy bedroom was nothing more than a movie set—a backdrop for her imagination, and the rest of the house hadn't been touched for months."

"But why not a basement?"

"Just a hunch. Besides, the carpet in her bedroom was wet—not much, but enough to soak into my jeans that first night when I got down on the floor to look under the bed. And if that fancy canopy hadn't been in the way I bet we would have seen stains on the ceiling. Remember, I heard water dripping."

"Maybe the roof leaked," she suggested. "It was an old house, and like you said, no one has tended to it in years."

"No doubt the roof did leak, but it hasn't rained anywhere near here for weeks. Nope," I insisted, "rain is out. My guess is there was a small bathroom or kitchenette in the attic with leaky plumbing."

"You're making all this up!" she accused.

"Maybe," I admitted honestly. "We'll just have to ask Beth when we find her."

"Here we go again!"

The afternoon was beautiful—the air sweet and fresh, with a warmth that was just a hint of the long hot summer to come. I didn't really want to go home and, I decided, neither did my daughter.

"How about a cup of coffee from your shop?"

"Coffee? You?"

"Yes," I insisted. "Some of that fancy blend with cinnamon and hazelnuts and raspberries—all of that artificial stuff—and lots of heavy cream and sugar."

"You just want dessert," she accused, and rightly so.

When Cassie came back to Rowan Springs after her graduation from Emory University, she surprised us all by announcing she was home to stay. I had expected her to go to work in some fancy glass tower in any one of the world's major cities. After all, she spoke three languages and could have easily made her way anywhere; but she insisted that Kentucky was her spiritual home—there was no need to waste time and money by going elsewhere. I didn't argue. Why bother when I had my heart's desire.

Cassie very independently made her own way. She took a job at the local coffee shop and saved enough to buy the business and add a bookstore when the owner left town. Originally her plan was to live in the apartment upstairs, but she decided to live with us instead. Mother took the rent Cassie paid each month to slowly upgrade her quarters, making them as private as possible. We fantasized that she would stay with us forever, but we knew our days with Cassie were numbered and we resolved to make the most of them.

I loved her little bookstore-cum-coffee shop. So did a lot

of people in town. It was the perfect spot for the business folk to meet every weekday morning for a cup of fresh hot coffee or tea and the latest news—either from the morning papers or the grapevine. Cassandra's Book Nook was especially popular that first winter with logs burning merrily in the big old-fashioned stone fireplace, lots of comfy overstuffed chairs, and a bottomless pot of hot mulled cider to attract patrons. When business fell off in the spring as customers began to prefer the out-of-doors, Cassie knocked down the back wall and created a charming brick patio that featured a fountain like the one from her childhood. On pleasant days like today, the graceful wooden benches she had arranged to give the maximum of privacy to each customer were usually full, but I was in luck: there was one vacant in my favorite shady spot.

Mindy, the petite blonde teenager who worked for Cassie, cornered her as soon as we crossed the threshold. The girl was positively quivering with excitement.

"Cassie! Oh, my God!" she squealed like a little blonde mouse. "Thank goodness! I've been frantic!"

Cassie was used to Mindy's "the sky is falling" attitude. "Slow down, honey," she urged calmly. "Take a deep breath—and then tell me what's wrong."

"Wrong? Oh, my God! Nothing's wrong!" the girl exclaimed with a huge grin. "It's just all so exciting! Aliens have landed in Rowan Springs! The whole town is talking about it. Can you just imagine? Here in Rowan Springs, of all places! Aliens with huge purple feet!"

I grabbed my cup of coffee from Cassie's outstretched hand and headed for the patio. I managed to make it all the way to my bench before I started laughing.

"Mindy told you about the aliens, I see."

I turned around and parted the leaves of a Japanese maple to see Bruce Hawkins sitting on the bench behind me. He was manfully plowing through the New York Times.

"Why do I have the unsettling feeling that this whole implausible story has something to do with you?" he asked.

"Little ole me?"

He leaned over my bench and pointed at my hairy purple bedroom slippers. "Yes, Paisley, little ole you."

I laughed and took a sip of my coffee. "You're sharp, but

not that sharp. You've been talking to Andy Joiner, haven't you?"

"Guilty as charged," he said with a sheepish grin.

"Damn it! Andy swore he'd keep my little, er, difficulty to himself."

Bruce folded up his paper and walked around to sit beside me. He had been a good-looking boy when we were in high school, and he was even better looking now. His light brown hair had receded only a fraction, his waistline was still trim, and his forget-me-not blue eyes as soulful as ever.

"Don't be mad at Andy," he said, shaking his head. "He figured you wouldn't be able to keep your nose clean. He said you might have need of my services." His smile faded, and he put on his courtroom face. "Andy says you're holding out on him. He says you saw something last night—something that really scared you. What's going on, Paisley?"

"Speaking of keeping your nose clean, what are you doing hanging around my sweet baby girl all day long?"

I watched in amusement as the area above his starched white collar and neat Windsor knot turned a dusky red. The color crawled up his face and settled on his cheeks before he was calm enough to answer.

"For heaven's sake, Paisley! What do you think I am?" he sputtered.

"I asked you first. Are you a philandering, skirt-chasing, cradle-robbing jerk, or do you have some other excuse for being a bookstore groupie?"

"I...I'm keeping an eye on someone. And for your information, it's for Cassie's own good. I happen to be very fond of that young lady."

I raised a skeptical eyebrow.

"In a fatherly kind of way, and you know it!" Bruce paused and stared at me intently for a moment. "You only said that to get me off the track, didn't you?" he laughed, blotting his damp upper lip with a snowy white handkerchief. "Wow, you had me going there for a minute. Ever think of becoming a lawyer? I could use a partner."

"Who?"

"Who, what?"

"Who are you keeping an eye on?"

"What threw you into such a panic last night that you practically begged to be arrested?" he countered.

"Coffee's good," I observed, as if he hadn't spoken.

"Maybe that's why I spend so much time here," he suggested.

"Yeah, right!"

We called off the verbal fencing match by unspoken mutual agreement and enjoyed a pleasant conversation while finishing our coffee. Bruce confided that his wife was indeed expecting and they were looking for a bigger house.

I laughed. "You and Mary have been looking for a bigger house since forever."

"Yes, but now she's nesting and her determination scares even me. What did you see last night, Paisley?"

"I thought we...?"

"Billy Martin said you practically climbed up his neck. By the way, he didn't mean to zap you with his Taser."

"You could'a fooled me."

"He feels pretty lousy about it, and his wife is giving him fits. She's a big fan of your books. Honestly, Paisley, I have my own reasons for thinking you're holding out on Andy."

"You tell me yours and I tell you mine," I suggested with a wicked leer.

Bruce looked around and saw that we were alone on the patio; nevertheless, he leaned closer and lowered his voice to a whisper before he spoke.

"A client of mine...."

"Who must remain nameless," I finished for him.

"Exactly," he added without so much as a smile. "My anonymous client received several—he called them 'hints' from Bethlehem Davis—hints that he come up with quite a tidy sum or she would present his wife with certain embarrassing details of a rather sordid little interlude in his life."

"Wow! Beth Davis is into blackmail?"

A worried frown creased Bruce's handsome face. "Careful, Paisley!" he cautioned. "Keep your voice down." He started to get up, spilling all ten sections of the newspaper on the patio. "This was a mistake," he said, shaking his head. "I shouldn't be sharing this with you—with anybody for that matter, but especially not with you."

I knelt down and hurriedly picked up the paper. I held it close to my chest like a ransom, hoping I could keep him from leaving.

"I figured it was something like this," I lied. "Everything pointed to it."

"Everything?" He sat back down on the bench, ignoring the newspaper. "What's 'everything'?"

I searched my mind desperately for old movie plots, Leonard's exploits—anything that might make Bruce think I already knew enough that it wouldn't matter if he told me more.

"Well, there's her bedroom for starters," I suggested mysteriously.

Bruce sat back on the bench and stretched his long legs in front of him. The polished gleam of his immaculate loafers made me acutely aware that I was still wearing my bedroom slippers. I tucked them underneath my seat and faced Bruce with what I hoped was a confident smile.

"Don't you...?" I started, but he held his hand up to stop me.

"Lavender walls, a big bed with lots of red velvet and gold tassels?" he asked.

I was stunned. "How did you know that?"

"Photographs, and a particularly nauseating video tape." He ran his fingers through his hair and sighed deeply, then turned to face me. His clear blue eyes were the window to a fine and honest soul. I felt like a louse for tricking him into talking.

"Look, Bruce," I began.

"My client has reason to believe there are more," he interrupted softly.

"More tapes, or more photos?" I asked, my guilt forgotten.

"More victims."

CHAPTER THIRTEEN

Cassie and I had one of our rare arguments on the way home from her shop.

"Beth isn't that sinister, Mom. You said yourself that she reminds you of Petunia Pig."

"What about Baby Face Nelson, or Billy the Kid, hummm? They didn't look all that sinister, either, did they?"

"Give it up, Mom! I'm tired of your constant references to those silly old black and white movies. And beside, it doesn't matter. I'm right!" She parked the Lincoln in the carriage house and unhooked her seat belt before she turned to confront me. "Why are you so intent on making Beth Davis a bad guy? Is it because Gran liked her manuscript and yet she's so disapproving of Leonard's books?"

"Oh, for goodness sakes, Cassie! You really think I'm that spiteful and petty?"

"Well...?"

I got out and slammed the car door a trifle harder than was necessary. The end of the seat belt caught in the crack, and I could hear the warning signal bleeping insistently behind me as I stalked angrily up the driveway to the house.

Mother was seated at my father's desk in the library engaged in an animated phone conversation. I knew Cassie would probably join her there or sit on the back porch, so I headed for the solitude of my moon garden on the other side of the house.

That spring had been filled with long gentle rains and mild temperatures—perfect conditions for the lilies, gardenias and roses now blooming in such profusion. I sat on the long white, wrought iron bench Mother had gifted me with the night I had planted the last rose bush, and breathed deeply of the fragrance surrounding me. I had been lucky. Every single expensive antique rose had thrived in this sunny and very fertile spot where a chicken house had stood many years ago.

Earlier in the year I had erected a graceful latticed arbor in the corner where my silver gazing ball sat on a slender pedestal. The four jasmine vines I planted in expectation that they would climb the trellis and eventually cover it with tiny, fragrant, little white stars were coming along nicely. All in all, I decided, my white moon garden was a huge success.

I relaxed against the back of the bench, gratified to feel the anger and tension of the day begin to ebb. This was my favorite time of the evening—just before sunset, when streaks of gold and scarlet paint the horizon and the first stars twinkle in the deep indigo sky above.

"Star light, star bright, first star I see tonight," I whispered, stopping because I never could remember the rest of the little poem that ended in a wish. Besides, I didn't know what to wish for. I was blessed with good health, moderate success, and the company of loved ones—even if I happened to be somewhat miffed with them at the moment. What more could a girl wish for, I wondered. A wee small voice deep inside my lonely heart begged to be heard, but I refused to listen. I was as happy as a piggy in mud—no need for foolish wishes.

"My dear, you look so innocent and peaceful sitting there surrounded by your lovely flowers—one would never know you were really a visitor from outer space."

Horatio was wearing a smart black evening suit that was just this side of a tuxedo. He looked particularly suave and handsome. I told him so when he took a seat beside me.

"Thank you, Paisley. I do feel somewhat festive tonight. I'm asking for your mother's hand once again. Wish me luck."

I chuckled. "How many times does this make?"

"Who knows," he answered with an extravagant shrug. "Who cares? I will pursue her affections with the last breath in my body."

I took the chilled Chardonnay he proffered, and touched the rim of his glass with mine. "Good luck, then," I saluted. "Although, as far as affection goes, I'm sure you already have hers."

His smile in the deepening twilight was as wistful as my mood.

"Perhaps, my dear. Perhaps." He took a sip of wine, savoring the bouquet before he spoke again. "Your dear late father is quite an act to follow. Although I'm sure I don't have to tell you that."

"John Sterling was something special, all right," I agreed with a fond smile.

"Men of his ilk are very rare. I recognized his qualities right away, of course. That's why I left for Europe and took myself out of the equation. If ever two people were suited for one another...."

He finished his wine and set the glass gently on the bench next to him. "Nonetheless, I shall continue with my quest for your mother's hand until she agrees, for agree she must!"

"How did you find out about the alien thing," I asked, changing the subject.

"Cassandra filled me in on the gruesome details. She seems to think you are vilifying Bethlehem Davis for no justifiable reason."

"I couldn't tell her everything, Horatio. And I can't tell you, either. I promised Bruce Hawkins I would keep his confidence." I finished my wine and let the glass dangle between my fingertips. "Even us aliens have some integrity."

"Young Hawkins told you about the blackmail scheme, didn't he?"

"You know?" I asked in surprise.

"I have for quite some time. It would seem that men who allow themselves to be caught in compromising situations are almost always compelled to relate their follies to someone else." His smile in the rapidly approaching dusk was ironic and slightly bitter. "Apparently, I have acquired a certain reputation over the years for listening without casting stones. That dubious quality seems to invite confession from all sorts of riff-raff."

"Somehow I didn't think you entertained riff-raff," I observed with a smile.

Horatio sighed and flicked a daring lightning bug off his elegant sleeve.

"Rowan Springs is a small town, Paisley. The longer you live here, the more alliances you will make. And you will discover that many of them are historical—handed down from the previous generation. Those loyalties are the hardest to ignore, even if the offspring are nothing more than weak and puny imitations of their fathers."

"So you listen."

"So I listen."

"Yuck!"

"Quite!" he agreed.

"How many times have you listened?"

"Three."

"Busy little lady, our Beth."

"So it would seem. Although things have taken on a different tenor over the past few months."

"How so?" I asked, as I stood to massage the leg that had gone to pins and needles from sitting too long on the hard bench.

"The request for filthy lucre is a new ingredient," said Horatio thoughtfully.

"What did she want before?"

"Invitations, introductions, access—commodities which can be more valuable than money to someone who knows how to make the most of them."

"What do you suppose brought about the change?" I asked.

"A new partner in crime, I think—one a good deal more unsavory than our Miss Davis." Horatio stood and brushed at the perfect pleat in his trousers. "Of course, I can't be sure of that, but I've read the blackmail notes. There's another voice there—a dangerous one, if I'm not mistaken."

We walked slowly around the house to the screen door of the back porch. Cassie was inside sitting spread-eagle on the flagstone floor playing with Aggie. We stood outside for a moment watching their rambunctious game. It was a charming picture: the beautiful young girl and her cute fuzzy dog.

"Be careful, my dear," said Horatio in a hushed voice. "You have a great deal to lose."

My feelings were still smarting from our earlier argument, so after I said goodnight to Horatio I went straight to my room without speaking to Cassie, or even Mother when I passed her in the kitchen. I felt sorry almost immediately because mother looked particularly lovely in an elegant sheath of pale ivory satin.

I decided to return and tell her so. After, all, I thought, this might be a very special night and I didn't want to do anything that might spoil it

"They've already gone," said Cassie. "Horatio had early dinner reservations somewhere special. He wouldn't even tell me where."

"Hernando's hideaway, probably," I muttered.

"There you go again," she sighed petulantly.

"For your information that's not an old movie! And neither was Baby Face Nelson, or Billy the Kid. They were real live, honest to goodness people—well, not so honest, maybe—but real, nevertheless. Perhaps you should spend more time studying twentieth century American history and less time making fun of your mother."

Aggie had been sitting protectively in front of Cassie watching my every move. When I pointed an innocent finger at my daughter while making my case, the dog launched herself at my ankle. She took two quick and painful nips before running into the house to hide.

"Damn, damn, and double damn!" I shouted as I hopped around the porch on one foot. "That rotten, cowardly little beast!" I flopped down on the chaise and pulled down my sock to inspect the latest dog bite.

Cassie leaned over to take a peek. "You're lucky," she observed coolly. "The skin's not even broken."

"You mean, she's lucky, don't you? Remember—I said one more bite, and she's toast?"

Cassie sat back on her heels and looked up at me. "You don't really mean that, Mom. You love Aggie as much as I do."

"Oh, yeah? Well, that's news to me!"

"You're just mad at me, and you're taking it out on poor little Aggie," she accused unjustly.

"So! First I'm petty and spiteful, and now I'm being unfair. Have I got that right?"

"Yes," answered my daughter with the tiniest of smiles. "But I'll forgive you—if you tell me everything Bruce said about Beth Davis."

"You little brat! How did you find out about that?" I laughed.

She unfolded her long legs and rose in one graceful motion. "Want some more wine?" she asked. "Horatio left the bottle."

"Sure," I grinned—happy that our fight was in the past. "And," I called after her, "bring something to munch on if you want me to talk"

She handed me a glass of wine and put a platter of celery hearts, carrot sticks and dip within reach at the end of the chaise.

"That's nothing but rabbit fodder," I complained. "I need real calories."

"The dip has two calories. Eat all you want," she said, crunching away.

I was hungry. And I had to admit that I been feeling better since Cassie instituted my new dietary regimen. I stopped complaining and ate.

"Umm," I said over a mouthful of carrot. "That dip is good."

"Confession is good for your soul, Mom, so redeem yourself. Tell me what Beth Davis is up to and maybe I won't keep on thinking you're a rotten, stinking, person."

I looked up and saw her mischievous grin and the twinkle in her eye. "How *did* you find out?" I asked, realizing that somehow she knew almost as much as I did.

"I eavesdropped," she admitted unashamedly. "When Horatio said he was taking you a glass of wine, I sneaked around to the guest wing and opened the sitting room window just a crack. I couldn't hear everything, but I heard enough to know I might owe you an apology."

CHAPTER FOURTEEN

Playing "good cop" some times, and "bad cop" at others, my daughter soon extracted every scrap of information I had withheld from her. When she finished, I was exhausted—and relieved that I no longer had to worry about giving something away. I was also starving. The bunny food platter had been licked clean, and I now wanted something more substantial.

"In the past," I began, "I would have invited you to join me in a fat-laden, cholesterol-filled, grease covered cheeseburger, but even I don't want that any more."

"Hooray," she shouted, doing an impromptu little victory dance.

"However," I interrupted, "I do require something more substantial than carrots, and I want it as soon as possible. Any suggestions?"

In just fifteen minutes by the kitchen clock Cassie had whipped up a delicious black bean veggie burger on a wheat bun with oven-baked potatoes, pickles, and thick slices of Vidalia onion and beefsteak tomato.

"Oh, my, Cassie! This is heavenly! Wherever did you find this stuff?"

"There's a new place in town, Mom. It's called a supermarket. You should give it a try sometime."

"Very funny!"

I rinsed the dishes and put them in the dishwasher while Cassie filled Aggie's water bowl and took her for a short walk. We met in the library—each taking up residence on one of the two comfortable sofas in front of the fireplace. Both French doors were open and the occasional evening breeze stirred the hems of the heavy draperies restlessly like the long skirts of indecisive ladies.

After asking Cassie if she minded, I turned off the Chinese porcelain lamp on the sofa table. I wanted to watch the moon rise over the treetops.

"How about a candle instead?" she suggested lazily. "There's a one of those big fat ones on the hearth."

She sounded totally relaxed so I got up and found the candle and the box of long fireside matches.

"Candlelight is so romantic," she sighed.

I curled back up on the sofa cushions, thinking that moonlight had candles beat all to hell, but then what did I know.

"Do you suppose," mused Cassie, "that Gran and Horatio have slept together, yet?"

"Good grief, Cassie!" I sputtered, thankful for the darkness that hid the girlish blush on my cheeks.

"Why shouldn't they have sex?" she asked innocently.

I thought about the decades that separated my daughter's generation and that of my mother—years filled with changes that made it difficult for either of them to understand the attitudes of the other. I decided to take a stab at an explanation despite the warning bells going off in the periphery of my mind.

"Fred Astaire, that's why."

"Here we go with the old movie shtick again!" she complained.

"Just give me a minute," I begged. "Maybe you'll understand Gran—and even me—a little better."

Her silence gave me all the permission I needed to launch my lecture. "Fred Astaire...."

"Was a skinny, funny-looking, practically bald old guy who danced around with his hands in his pockets. Now, how romantic is that?" she interrupted.

I didn't have to see the sneer to know it was there. "Cassie, do you mind?"

"Oh, all right," she grumbled.

"It was the dream...," I began.

"Pardon?"

"If you will just give me a chance?" I snapped, throwing a needlepoint pillow in her direction. "He *was* a funny-looking, skinny old guy, I agree. But he stirred the imagination of every woman who watched him swirl around the dance floor. Those years of war and financial hardship were difficult in the real world, but on the big screen, life was beautiful, and for one hour and thirty-four minutes every woman in the audience could pretend to be in Fred's arms—to be dressed in gorgeous clothes—to come and go from the theater in a limousine, and to step out of the chorus line and become a star."

"And the romance?" she yawned.

"I'm coming to that," I told her patiently. "It was never spoken—never 'in your face' like it is today. There were hints: eyes cast in a certain direction, a rose left on a pillow, an anonymous love letter—that made the heroine dream of a kiss stolen by a masked man in the moonlight. And that was the epitome, the high point of the affair. There was no bedroom scene—no sweaty groping under the sheets. It was delicate and sensitive, and...."

"Boring!" interjected Cassie.

"Not at all!" I insisted. "Quite the contrary. That kiss—that beautiful kiss in the moonlight, with the orchestra swelling in the background as the hero rode away on his magnificent horse—or sailed away on his pirate ship—or swung across the jungle on a vine—made your heart pound with excitement. And translated into everyday life—you sat in that theater with a pimply-faced boy sitting next to you, hoping for nothing more than that first tentative touch of his hand on yours. And when your hero finally did get up the nerve to grasp your sweaty palm—it was as if your souls joined those of the lovers on the screen. And believe me, Cassie, there's nothing boring about sharing a life with Katherine Hepburn and Spencer Tracy for an hour and a half."

When she made no response, I sat up on my knees and squinted across the room in the candlelight. "Cassie?"

My daughter was sound asleep and snoring softly, but I was right and I knew it. And if Cassie had heard anything I said it was worth the effort. I slipped down in the corner of the sofa and closed my eyes to dream of D'Artagnan and the other Musketeers.

I'm not sure which sound woke me up—the sputtering of the candle in the wind, or the metallic scrape of the screen door opening. I lay still, trying to decide what was the best course of action. Should I jump up and scream, or pretend to be asleep until I saw the intruder. My inactivity solved the problem. The dark shadow moved inside so fast that I had no choice but to lie there, paralyzed by fear. It was the same dark-robed figure I had seen in Beth's kitchen. I struggled against the mental chains that held me, and finally breaking loose, I screamed.

"Mom! Mom! What's wrong?" shouted Cassie as she shook me awake.

"Wha...?"

"You were screaming. Did you have a bad dream?" she asked, her voice filled with gentle concern.

I wiped the sweat off my upper lip with a shaking hand and pulled myself to a sitting position. "I...I guess so," I stammered.

"Well, you certainly scared me to death! And poor little Aggie went running. If you're sure you're okay, I'll go see about her."

With enormous effort, I withheld my absolutely negative opinion of Aggie as a watchdog and gave my daughter a reassuring smile. "Go, Honey. I'm fine, really."

When Cassie left, I stood on trembling legs and took a deep breath. Moonlight now flooded the room—outlining every object so clearly that it was a moment or so before I realized the candle had indeed gone out. I glanced quickly at the screen door and sighed with relief when it appeared to be closed. Not until I got closer did I see that it really was standing open about three inches—wedged open with a small rock placed between the jamb and the bottom of the door.

"What the hell?"

I knelt down to examine the rock more closely and never saw the creep who clobbered me from behind.

When I opened my eyes again, struggling out of the dark fog of my dreams, I saw Cassie and Mother and Horatio hovering over me.

"Oh, thank God!" sobbed Mother. "Paisley, darling, are you all right?"

"Wasss...," I croaked, then cleared my throat and tried again. "What's going on?"

I was not in my own wonderfully cozy bed with the luxurious silk comforter and soft pink sheets—that much I knew for sure. These sheets were scratchy—something my mother would never stand for, and the mattress made funny plastic noises when I moved.

"Don't try to sit up, Mom," cautioned Cassie. "Dr. D. wants you to stay absolutely still until he sees your X-rays."

"X-rays? X-rays of what? Will somebody please tell me what's going on?"

CHAPTER FIFTEEN

Saijad answered my questions while I pretended to eat a cold hospital breakfast of green eggs and something indescribable that definitely was not ham—or anything else I had ever seen before.

"I think you were hit over the head with a blunt object, little sister," explained Saijad. "An object very much like the one which also did damage to your friend Miss Davis—who stayed in this very room, by the way."

I gulped down a mouthful of eggs, trying not to taste them. "Yeah? No kidding?" I looked around with sudden interest as it occurred to me that Beth had probably left her things behind when she vanished from the hospital. "Where's the lost and found department, Saijad?"

He turned and gave me a stern, impatient look—well, a look that was intended to be stern and impatient. Saijad merely looked like an excited puppy that wasn't getting enough attention. He pointed to the series of X-rays he was holding up to the light.

"Do you not want to know about your injuries, little sister?" he asked in his most professional voice.

"Injuries? I thought...you didn't say I had any injuries!" I accused with alarm.

Instantly contrite, Saijad dropped the X-ray films on the chair and hastened to my bedside.

"No, Paisley, you have no injuries," he assured me. "A bruise, nothing more. Your hair...well, it is true that your hair is very...."

"Go on," I laughed with relief—amused by his gallant attempt at diplomacy.

"Your hair protected you from further harm, little sister,

because it is so, er...."

"So...what?" I urged wickedly.

A faint blush darkened his handsome features as he searched for words to describe my wild and tousled hair as tactfully as possible.

"So carefree and natural, of course! And thick! That's what saved you—your hair is quite luxuriant—otherwise, you might have had a true concussion, like Miss Davis."

I smiled knowingly at my friend.

"I congratulate you, Saijad. Your knowledge of the English language is impeccable, and besides that, you are absolutely the most charming man I know."

"Mercy!" he exclaimed with a pleased smile on his face. "Even more charming than the debonair Horatio Raleigh?"

I threw back the covers on my bed and swung my knees over the side.

"Let's just say you and Horatio would finish neck and neck on Derby Day." I looked around the bare hospital room. "Where are my clothes?"

He watched me solemnly for a moment, his smile turning upside down—then burst my bubble.

"I cannot allow you to leave, Paisley," he said sadly.

I was truly astonished. "Why ever not?"

"It is hospital protocol," he explained. "The patient must remain at least twenty-three hours after a head injury—for observation."

I smiled as brightly as I could, even though I could feel the beginnings of a pounding ache behind my left ear.

"How 'bout I observe myself all afternoon in my own little bed. Cassie can even sit and observe with me."

"Sorry, Paisley. Please to get back in bed and relax. I am ordering something for that headache."

"How did you...?"

"And they are bringing lunch very soon. You are most lucky. It is the day they serve meat loaf and blue Jell-O." Saijad hastily waved goodbye as he slipped out into the hospital corridor, closing the door firmly behind him.

I eased back into bed, resting my aching head carefully on the hard pillow. I hated being ill and dependent. My head hurt and I felt pitifully sorry for myself. I didn't even try to stop the warm tears as they oozed out from underneath my eyelids. I was about to work myself up into a good hard cry when the door opened abruptly and an aggressively cheerful, overly plump nurse bounced in like a pink and white beach ball. I was beginning to see why Beth had blown this joint at the earliest opportunity.

"Hello, hello, hello!" chortled the woman. "Are we feeling better this afternoon? Hmm?"

She put a plastic food tray on the bedside table, then dug a syringe out of her pocket and held it up to the light.

"Saijad didn't say anything about an injection!" I protested.

"Perhaps not to you," she said condescendingly. "But Dr. Dhanvantari," she emphasized the formal address, "ordered something to relax us."

"Well," I quipped. "I don't need relaxing, so it must be for you."

She flashed me a practiced nursing school smile that never quite reached her hard, unfriendly eyes.

"Look, Missy, I have four other patients on this floor and no time for mollycoddling, so roll over and show us your bottom."

With the small, economic gestures used by many heavy people she demonstrated the moves I should make. I couldn't help myself—despite my overwhelming desire not to be used like a pincushion by this erstwhile Florence Nightingale, I started laughing.

"Ow!"

"I've taken care of bigger trouble than you, Missy," she said with a steely smile as she withdrew the needle from my bare hip. "Now! Let's eat our lunch before it gets cold like our breakfast did."

She pulled the tray trolley up over to my bed and removed the metal dome from the luncheon plate.

"Ummm, yum! You're in luck! Meatloaf and smashy potatoes."

I stared at the gray square of congealing fat, and what appeared to be a small mound of library paste.

"Yum."

"And blue Jell-O! This is my favorite day of the week,"

grinned my greedy "Florence." "I just hope you haven't delayed me too long. Last Thursday one old hag wouldn't let me give her a bed bath and I missed my lunch."

She gave me a look intended to forestall any further problems. It did. I had dealt with kidnappers, drug dealers, and murderers; but this woman really scared me—besides, there was that needle.

She grabbed my wrist and mashed my pulse point for a minute while she gave a perfunctory glance at her watch, then forced a fork in my hand.

"Eat up!" she ordered. "I'll be back for that empty plate in half and hour."

I rubbed my wrist and stuck my tongue out at the door as it swung shut—half afraid that she would somehow know and come back inside to punish me. When I was sure she had gone, I pushed the tray back and got out of bed. Nothing in the world—not even Nurse Ratchet—could make me eat that plateful of lard—it was going in the toilet.

I turned to grab the tray and had to grab hold of the headboard instead. My legs had turned into rubber. The first thought I had was that Saijad had missed something—perhaps I had some brain damage, after all—then I remembered the injection and realized it had to be the medication.

I lay back down and closed my eyes while I waited for the room to quit spinning. I don't know how much time passed, but when I heard someone outside in the corridor, I panicked. The nurse and her needle had assumed monumental proportions in my drug influenced imagination and I felt I had to avoid her wrath at all costs. I reached out and grabbed the lunch plate and dumped its contents in the drawer of the bedside table on top of the Gideon bible and a box of handy-wipes.

Cassie peeked in the door and scooted quickly inside.

"Mom?" she laughed when she saw the guilty look on my face. "What's going on?"

Cassie stayed with me all afternoon while I drooled and giggled and tried desperately to remember what it was that I wanted her to do. We played twenty questions with hilarious results, but nothing came to mind.

Andy Joiner sauntered in around three, bringing me a milkshake and wearing a sheepish grin. I sipped my malted milk and tried to concentrate on the conversation since it concerned what had happened last night, but for the life of me I couldn't seem to assimilate the fact that Andy thought it was nothing more than an accident. Apparently, neither could Cassie.

"But Saijad said the blow was from a blunt instrument," protested my daughter.

"And you said yourself, Cassie, that she had a bad dream and appeared disoriented."

Cassie nodded reluctantly while I grinned idiotically at the two of them.

"It's a bit odd, don't you think, that Paisley's story about an intruder is exactly like the dream she had?"

"Well...yes, I guess so. But, Mom is usually not...."

"Cassie, we all have our weaker moments—especially as we get older," he observed with a wicked smile in my direction. "I checked that house from top to bottom," Andy continued. "There was no sign of forced entry, nor was there any 'blunt instrument' except for the corner of the door frame which, by the way, had strands of Paisley's hair caught in screen. It's obvious to me that she got up too quickly, lost her balance, and fell into the door. I can't justify any more time investigating what I consider to be an accident pure and simple."

Cassie spent the rest of the afternoon trying to convince me that Andy didn't really mean I was decrepit and senile, but I wouldn't stop crying until she pointed out that he and his wife, Connie, were five years older than I, and would no doubt be in a home for the elderly and infirmed while I was still cavorting nimbly around town. Exhausted and frazzled, she finally kissed me good night and went home to see about Aggie.

I came down from my prescription narcotic high just in time to take my sleeping pill from a nicer, but even more insistent nurse. I spat it back out and tucked it in the drawer on top of the "smashy potatoes" as soon as she was gone; but this nurse was clever—she peeked in on me every few minutes causing me to keep my eyes closer longer than I would have wished. The result of this, of course, was that I fell asleep just as if I had taken the pill in the first place.

I woke up a few hours before dawn, clear-headed and drug

free, and remembered immediately what I had wanted Cassie to do; but since she probably wouldn't have time to look for Beth's abandoned clothes in the hospital's lost and found when she came to pick me up, I would have to find them before she got here.

My headache had faded away, leaving me with nothing more than a tenderness above my hairline and a slight ringing in my ears. I vaguely remembered Saijad reassuring me at some point that both were temporary conditions. A slight dizziness was the only other symptom I experienced as I tiptoed into the adjoining bath and quietly splashed cold water on my face.

A brief glance in the mirror told me more than I wanted to know about my physical condition. My hair stood up in undisciplined auburn corkscrews and the pale lavender shadows that encircled my green eyes gave me the surprised look of a pastel Panda. I told myself that I felt better than the mirror said, and resolutely ignored the chorus of midget insects humming loudly in my ears.

The closet door slid open without a squeak, but there was nothing inside for me to wear, not even a regulation hospital robe. "Damnation," I whispered as I rose up too quickly, setting off a raucous chain reaction of rattling metal coat hangers. "Saijad's responsible for this! I can't believe that sneaky rascal didn't trust me!"

I slumped down on the edge of the bed, annoyed by the knowledge that even I wouldn't dare skulk around the main lobby of the hospital with my bare butt hanging out. Somehow I would have to delay my discharge so Cassie would have time to check out the lost and found. We might make it work if Mother didn't come along to see me safely home. She was just way too organized and efficient. I would be halfway to Meadowdale Farm before I could say "goodbye and thank you kindly" to my gentle nurses.

The ringing in my ears had ceased at some point, and now I could clearly hear the grumbling of my empty stomach. I crawled under the scratchy sheet, suddenly needing the meager warmth it provided. The plastic cover on the thin mattress protested loudly with my every movement, but on the other side of the door, the hospital was still and quiet.

I looked at the digital clock on the bedside table and was

surprised to see how late it was. In just two hours the seven to three shift would come on duty—Nurse Ratchet would be back. I considered cleaning the potatoes out of the drawer and decided against it. Let her explain it away.

I was hungry, but not hungry enough to eat any of that cafeteria slop. The doctors always got plenty of sugary, greasy doughnuts to see them through the night—Saijad had once told me that was the reason he didn't mind working the graveyard shift. If the doctor's lounge was close to my room I might be able to sneak a quick Krispy-Kreme and a cup of coffee.

Doughnuts and hot java suddenly became the most important things in my life. I had to have them no matter what. I slithered out of bed and over to the door, opening it a crack and listening intently for any signs of activity. The muffled sound of snores came from the room next to mine, but other than that, the corridor was silent and empty. I slipped though my door and down the hallway as quiet as Sandberg's fog—"on little cat feet." I passed three empty rooms on each side of the hall before I reached the closed door of the doctor's lounge. I took a deep breath and crossed my fingers as I boldly entered the room.

The unforgiving glare of the bright florescent ceiling light blinded me for a second while I stood there praying that I was alone. Reassured with the absence of laughter or rude remarks, I peeked out from under my eyelashes and fumbled around for the light switch. The harsh light immediately gave way to the soft glow of two squat little brass table lamps on either side of a comfortable overstuffed sofa, and the muted light over a bank of kitchen cabinets on one wall.

An expensive, state-of-the-art coffee machine on the counter beckoned. I grabbed a large paper cup and filled it with three spoons of sugar before I poured the hot coffee. I looked around and found the handle of a small under counter fridge and opened it up to a wealth of riches. Inside was a pint of coffee cream and a plate piled high with sandwiches. I grabbed a pimento cheese and a tuna salad and gobbled down the first while I stirred the cream into my coffee and looked around for more goodies. Sure enough, a large carton of Krispy-Kremes sat in the middle of a round table in the corner. I sighed with contentment as I swallowed the last of the tuna and reached for a jelly doughnut.

The coffee warmed me up and a mere two bites of the doughnut assuaged the last of my hunger. I curled up on the sofa and tucked my feet beneath me as I sipped a second cup and compared this cozy little space to my sterile hospital room.

I approved of the soft peach-colored walls and the dark green plush carpet. The damask sofa was nice and the lamps so-so, but the garish watercolor of a fleshy, over-grown gardenia hanging on the wall gave me the creeps. A lovely cherry armoire stood majestically in one corner. Tall and narrow, with four ornately carved doors, the armoire's stately appearance tickled my curiosity.

I finished my coffee, tossed my cup and the uneaten doughnut in the garbage, and went straight to the armoire. My mother's voice whispered admonitions in my ear about respecting the privacy of others the entire time it took to turn the big brass key in the lock and open the upper doors.

"Rats!" I don't know what I expected to find, but a twenty-seven inch television set didn't fit the bill. I closed the doors carefully and turned the lock—although what purpose the key served I couldn't imagine. I pulled half-heartedly at the doors down below.

Unexpectedly, I had to use the key once more, and found a VCR plus stacks of teaching tapes—herniorrhaphies, oophorectomies, and a myriad of other surgical procedures whose names I couldn't pronounce.

I was closing the doors when I noticed a brown paper bag tucked in the back. "Oh, what have we here?" I whispered with a wicked grin. "Tapes in a plain brown wrapper, I suppose. Naughty little doctors!"

I reached inside and tugged the bag out of its hiding place. Surprised to find that it was too light and squishy to hold cassettes, I carried my treasure back to the sofa and dumped its contents out on the cushion. Satin, feathers, and brightly colored sequins twinkled in the soft light—I had found Bethlehem Davis's belongings.

CHAPTER SIXTEEN

Cassie and Mother came to fetch me at eight-thirty sharp. Cassie handed me a plastic bag with fresh underwear and jeans, and Mother presented me with a lovely new silk blouse in a shade of lavender that perfectly matched the circles under my eyes. While they were talking to someone at the nurse's station, I pulled Beth's naughty nighties out from under my mattress and tucked them away in the bag Cassie had brought and then dressed quickly in my own blessed duds. We left by the side entrance without a word to anyone—even Saijad—since he was busy delivering triplets.

"Wow! Thank, God!" I exclaimed as we pulled out of the parking lot. "It's great to be out of that hell hole!"

"It cannot have been that bad, Paisley," argued Mother. "I'm told our little town hospital measures up quite well."

"Only if you like plastic mattresses and monster nurses! And don't even get me started on the food!"

"I saw you stuffing something in the bag, Mom. What did you steal? Some of those marvelous hospital towels, or maybe a sandpaper sheet?"

"Surely not!" exclaimed Mother.

"Don't worry, Mother," I grinned. "I found Beth's clothes, Cassie! They were hidden in the doctor's lounge. Somebody was probably getting their jollies out of playing with them between patients."

"Paisley! What a suggestion!"

"Well, Mother, why weren't they in the 'lost and found' department like they should have been?"

"Mom's right, Gran. And just wait until you see what your proper Miss Davis wears to catch her 'zzz's.'"

Mother reluctantly agreed with us when we displayed the

assortment of filmy nylon, satin, feathers and lace on the library desk.

"Oh, my!" she exclaimed with dismay. "They really are astonishing."

"And this lot is nothing compared to the rest of her stuff!" declared Cassie. "Honestly, Gran, she had drawers full of things way more revealing—crotchless panties, bosom tassels, G-strings, thongs...."

"That's quite enough, dear. I do believe you. But what could Beth have possibly have done with all those things?"

"You have to be kidding, Mother!"

"You mean?"

"Well, yes!"

I watched her patrician features turn a charming shade of crimson, then slowly fade to porcelain as she struggled for control.

"You have absolutely no proof of any such thing!" she declared.

I picked up a single purple plume and blew it in her direction. "Don't I?"

"I'm sorry, dear, but it will take more than a few feathers to prove to me that a modest young woman like Beth Davis is a...well...a woman of questionable repute. As far as her choice of wardrobe goes...why, everyone has their little peccadilloes, even I."

Cassie laughed delightedly as she held up a garish red satin bra with sequined nipples. "You call this a peccadillo, Gran?"

"Never mind that," I grinned. "This is too good to be true." I plopped down on the sofa, wincing as the tender spot on my head came into contact with the cushion. "Just what are these little peccadilloes of yours, Mother? Don't tell me you've taken to sleeping in the buff?"

"Of course not!" she denied heatedly. "You know perfectly well my feelings on that subject. I told you often enough when you were growing up: any number of things could happen during the nocturnal hours which would require one to be adequately dressed—a fire, a medical emergency, a natural disaster...."

"Then what are they?" insisted Cassie.

"What are what?" asked Mother absently, as she tucked an

errant wisp of silver-white hair back into place and straightened her pearls.

"Your peccadilloes," I reminded her with exaggerated patience. "Your granddaughter actually thinks you're going to slip up and reveal something intimate about yourself." Suddenly, I remembered Horatio's matrimonial plans. "Oh, my God!" I shouted, clapping my hands. "Speaking of revealing something intimate—what was your answer to Horatio's proposal?"

Mother stood abruptly and crossed over to the French doors—an action which effectively hid her face from us. "I would like a nice cup of tea," she said quietly. "How about you, Cassie, dear?"

"Sure, Gran, but what did...?"

"I'll have it ready in a jiffy," Mother said as she left the room without another word.

"Hummpf," I grunted. "Wha'cha think about dem apples?"

"She was very quiet last night," observed Cassie thoughtfully. "I blamed it on your little misadventure, but maybe it had more to do with Horatio than your accident. I wonder what happened."

"Unless she orders flowers and a wedding cake we may never know," I sighed. "Your grandmother is the most tight-lipped woman I ever knew."

"Not like us," laughed Cassie.

I grinned back at her. "No, not like us," I agreed. "It must be our Latin blood."

"You know what, Mom? All of these undies have the same labels."

"Yeah?"

"See," she said, pointing to a little heart-shaped tag on the fuchsia gown. "They're all from Lady Valentine's, whoever that is."

"Maybe we should make it our business to find out."

When Cassie bought the coffee shop, she also invested in a brand new computer with all the trimmings and went online with a virtual catalogue displaying her wares. Her web site had proved almost as successful as the coffee shop itself. While I took a shower and re-invented myself as a person, she went downtown to surf the net for "Lady Valentine."

She got back in time to join me for lunch on the back porch. I surprised her by making a salad with all of her favorites: Feta cheese, sprouts, sunflower seeds, romaine, and Kalamata olives.

"You're really beginning to get the hang of this food thing, Mom," she complimented with a smile. "Isn't Gran having lunch?"

I shrugged, trying to convey a levity I didn't really feel. Mother had not answered when I knocked on her sitting room door earlier. I was worried about her, but there was nothing I could do but wait until she was ready, or willing, to confide in me.

"What did you find out about Madame Valentine?" I asked in an effort to change the subject.

Cassie was quiet for a moment, then grabbed her big leather handbag and pulled out a notebook. "'Madame' is right," she laughed, "in a least one case, that is—Valentine's House of Desire, in Ketchikan, Alaska, which advertises 'the maximum of satisfied relaxation and'...."

"Yes, do go on," I prompted with a leer.

"Oh, nothing...just something nasty about the North Pole. I can't believe they got away with that on the Internet!"

"So who is our Valentine?" I prompted.

"Our Valentine's is a lingerie and gift shop for 'those special occasions.' And you'll never guess where it's located!"

"Enlighten me."

"On Highway 62—just outside of Morgantown in a strip mall near the army base."

"Figures."

Cassie grinned. "You up for a road trip? I'll drive if you're still 'disoriented'."

Lady Valentine's establishment was more of, well, more of everything than we could have ever imagined. At first glance, it was only a simple, square-shaped cement block building—what made it unusual was the bright and shiny coat of cotton-candy pink paint and the red neon hearts which pulsed with electronic arrhythmia around the edges of the roof.

"Wow!"

"Yeah," I agreed. "It looks like...."

"Mom! Be nice!"

"I am nice."

"You know what I mean. Be nice when we go inside. If you start making cute remarks, I'll leave—I swear!"

I worked up the sweetest, most innocent smile I could muster and advanced to the door of the shop just two steps behind my judgmental offspring. A band of corpulent pink cupids hand painted across the transom almost caused me to lose it, but I heeded Cassie's warning just in time to quell an incipient giggle.

The opening of the shop door must have triggered some recording device because we were greeted by the swelling, romantic strains of "Unchained Melody" as we entered.

"My God," I whispered. "It's like stepping inside a candy box."

"Mom!"

"Okay, okay."

But I was right. Frothy items covered with lace and satin ribbons decorated every corner and counter in the shop. Three tiered carousels filled with colorful silk under-things filled a center aisle that led through the shop to a huge satin canopied bed at the end. A sense of *déjà-vu* filled me as I realized that the bed in Beth's house had been modeled on this very one. Except for the color scheme—this one was in various shades and permutations of pink and reds—they were identical.

This time it was Cassie's turn to be amazed.

"Wow!" she whispered, her breath warm against my ear.

We both jumped when a pleasant voice called out.

"Hello, my dears! Welcome to my little shop. I can tell from the delighted wonder on your faces that this is your first visit to Lady Valentine's. How may I help you?"

The plump and pleasant looking woman could have been anyone's charming little grandmother. Bright blue eyes sparkled above rosy cheeks, a pert little nose, and a cupid's bow of a mouth. An expertly tinted blonde halo puffed out above her ears and made her seem taller than she actually was. She had further enhanced her presence by choosing a shiny silk caftan of gem-colored stripes shot with gold threads. She looked like a cross between Mrs. Pillsbury Doughboy, Sr., and a Christopher Radko Christmas tree ornament.

"Is there something I can help you with?" she repeated

with a winsome smile.

Her manner was so delightful, so appealing—I was completely mesmerized into making my first mistake.

"We need some information about purchases made in the last year by Bethlehem Davis," I announced naively, then watched in amazement as the woman shed her amiability like a snake sheds its skin—from the eyes down. Those bright blue orbs narrowed and grew cold as the soft contours of her body sharpened into angles and she assumed a hostile stance—ready to strike at a moments notice.

"Who wants to know? Who are you? You don't look like cops to me."

"Ah...we're not, cops, I mean. We're...ah, friends," I explained, after searching my brain rapidly for a plausible answer. "Beth has disappeared and we're trying to find her."

"How kind of you," she sneered.

"We're very worried about her, Lady Valentine. My grandmother...."

"And just who is your grandmother?" interrupted the woman angrily.

"Anna Howard Sterling," replied Cassie in a meek little voice.

The three little words that had gotten us *entrée* into so many places in the past worked their magic once again.

"John Sterling's wife," she said with the tiniest of smiles.

"*You* knew my grandfather?" gasped Cassie.

"Don't be so shocked, you pompous little twit!" ordered Lady Valentine, as the twinkle returned to her eyes and her smile broadened. "Come! I'll fix you a cup of tea and then decide if you're worth my time or not."

We followed in her shiny, iridescent wake as she led us through a curtain into a small kitchenette at the back of the shop. In just a few minutes she had a kettle boiling merrily on the stove and the two of us seated across from her at a cozy little kitchen table. She poured the water over tea leaves in a lovely china teapot and placed it on the table where she had already arranged dainty cups and saucers, and a plate of pink frosted heart-shaped sugar cookies.

"First of all," she began as she poured the tea through a silver strainer, "my name is Edna Brown, and my association with your grandfather was purely professional."

Cassie turned as pink as the cookie she had at her lips. "Wha...what do you mean?" she stammered.

Edna Brown stared at her for a second, then burst into a deeply appreciated belly laugh. Cassie turned even redder while I kept my mouth shut for once and enjoyed the moment.

Finally, Edna pulled herself together and wiped the tears from her eyes with a tiny white napkin as fine as any in my mother's linen chest. "Rest easy, child," she gasped. "Don't let your imagination run away from you. John Sterling was a fine man. I would be the last person to try and tarnish his reputation." She smiled again for the first time since I had put my foot in my mouth—only this time the smile was genuine. "Your grandfather helped my son get a football scholarship. Donnie was the first person in our family to have a chance at higher education. He would have made it, too," she added proudly.

I held my breath for the sad tidings I suspected would follow, but Edna surprised me once again.

"Donnie," she continued, "he took a job out West that summer before college and fell in love with the life out there. He took up roots, became a forest ranger, married a girl from Boulder. Now I have five, or is it six?—grandbabies. My son didn't take the road offered, but nevertheless, I can't thank John Sterling enough for giving a fatherless boy direction." She made a sudden move toward me. "So what do you want to know about Beth Davis?" she said, patting me on the cheek.

"Well, for starters," I responded. "What did she buy and when?"

"I could look it up for you to be absolutely sure, but my memory's as good as ever and if that will do...?"

"Absolutely," I encouraged, not wanting her to have any second thoughts.

"At first Beth was shy and tentative—quite modest in her purchases. Six months later she came back for a couple of my more exciting outfits...." Edna sat up straight and thrust out her bosom. She looked like a preening parakeet. "...then a few weeks after that she came back and quite boldly asked about certain bizarre items used in kinky bedroom activities. I made it quite clear to her that Lady Valentine deals in romance, not perversion," she sniffed. "But she didn't seem to mind. Said she would look on the Internet for the other stuff. Then she bought lots of my more, er, slinky outfits with feathers and sequins, and the bed things: satin sheets, pillowcases—all of that."

"*All of that* must have set her back a pretty penny," I suggested, hoping for Edna's appraisal of Beth's financial situation.

"You get what you pay for," she replied enigmatically. "When she first came in the shop I knew I had a customer for life. If ever a young woman lives in her head, that one does—I said to myself."

"When was that?" interrupted Cassie. "I mean, when did she first start coming here?"

Edna paused as she poured fresh tea into our cups. "Again, I'd have to check my books to be certain—but I'd almost be willing to swear it was twenty-six months and three days ago."

I laughed. "If that's a wild guess, it's pretty specific."

"It's not a guess, honey," she said with a grin. "I was just showing off. Lady Valentine's celebrated its second anniversary a little over two months ago. Beth Davis was one of my first customers."

"What do you mean by saying Beth 'lived in her head'?"

"I could tell by the way she dressed—the little things she did to try to and spice up her wardrobe. Paper flowers, butterflies—cheap and tacky, maybe; but she probably had visions of herself in a tropical garden wearing flowers behind her ears. And she was always kinda' quiet. Never tried anything on—just stared at things with a spacey look until she made her decisions. Then she took what she wanted in all three sizes—Nymphet, Enchantress, and Goddess."

"Which is?"

"Small, medium and large, of course."

"But, why all three?" asked Cass.

"Go figure! One of the reasons Lady Valentine's has been such a success is that Edna Brown never asks any questions. What I don't know pays the bills and the rest goes into my brokerage account."

I could tell from the sound of her voice that even though Edna Brown might be willing to tell us more, Lady Valentine was being politely dismissive. Not wanting to offend her in case we might have more questions at a later date, I took up her cue and rose to leave.

"Thanks for everything, Ms. er, Lady Valentine," said Cass, with a smile. "I really enjoyed looking around your shop. Maybe someday when I have more time...."

I placed an open palm in the small of my daughter's back and gave a her firm shove toward the door, reminding myself to have a discussion with her on the way home about what was appropriate in ladies lingerie.

CHAPTER SEVENTEEN

"You're hardly the last word on what is or isn't appropriate for a southern lady's underwear wardrobe, Mom!" observed my daughter.

"No, but your grandmother is, and I distinctly remember what she had to say on the subject when I was your age: absolutely nothing but white, ivory, or the palest pink."

"Humph!"

"Go ahead. Ask her!"

When she didn't keep up her end of our bantering I decided Cassie must have settled back for a catnap. She surprised me when she asked, "I guess our trip was wasted, huh?"

I pondered that point for a moment before I answered.

"Maybe not. It's always encouraging to see the entrepreneurial spirit succeed."

"Don't kid around, Mom. We don't know any more now than we did before we drove all the way over here."

"That's not exactly true. We found just one more in a long list of kind things your grandfather did for others, and one more person who remembers him with fondness. And we know that Beth had a tutor—or mentor—who was guiding her every move."

"Edna Brown?"

"Goodness, no. Someone else. A Svengali who took a timid little paper butterfly and step by step turned her into a blackmailing Mata Hari."

"You're making that up so this won't seem like a wild goose chase!"

"Deduction, my dear, Cassandra, deduction, pure and simple—and," I added enigmatically, "my recollection of something Horatio said the other night."

"What?"

"You were eavesdropping. Figure it out."

No matter how much she badgered me, I refused to tell Cassie what I was talking about. After a few fruitless guesses, she slumped down in her seat and took the nap I was counting on. I needed some quiet time to think.

I barely heard her soft snores as I went over my mental checklist. Fact number one: Bethlehem Davis was blackmailing, or extorting money from, or whatever the technical term was, at least three of Rowan Springs's "finest" citizens. Fact number two: before she asked for money, Beth merely wanted *entrée* into the inner circle of the movers and shakers in our fair city. Since nobody moves or shakes very much without Horatio knowing about it, I would have to get him to break down and name names. And I would have to find out what Beth held over their heads to make sense of facts number three through twenty—which encompassed everything from the disappearing manuscript to the fuchsia feathers still floating around inside Watson.

Cassie woke up just as we drove up to the house. The afternoon sun was low on the horizon and a few of the more daring bunnies were creeping out of the hedges for their dinner of the sweet clover that grew in profusion underneath the pear trees.

"Hungry?" I asked as I watched them play. "We can see if Gran wants to drive down to Sallie's."

"I'm pooped, Mom," she admitted. "I didn't sleep very well last night. I think I'll go finish my nap. You go ahead with Gran if you want."

I left Watson in the driveway and went in search of Mother. I finally found her sitting on the pretty wrought iron bench.

"Your moon garden really is quite lovely, Paisley."

"Thank, you," I said as I plopped down on the soft grass beside the bench.

"I've been sitting here for over an hour. The peace and quiet, it's so soothing. Like a balm to a troubled mind."

I turned quickly away from performing an aphid check on the bottom leaves of my newest rose bush. "Oh, God! What have I done now?"

She smiled and looked directly at me for the first time. "You?" she laughed. "Nothing, dear. Although you know how I feel about your wearing jeans all the time."

I sighed dramatically and lay back in the grass, my arms crossed behind my head for a pillow. "If I had anything else on I couldn't enjoy myself like this, and you'd be fussing about grass stains all the time like you used to when I was little."

It was her time to sigh—a quiet, sad little sound. "You're right, dear. I wasn't as understanding a mother with you and Velvet as you have been with our dear Cassandra."

"Wow!"

"Surprised that I will admit it?" she smiled. "I've been meaning to tell you that for some time now." She shook her head gently. "Why is it we always put off saying the really important things?"

She nervously fingered the pearls at her throat before she continued. "My mother used to tell me that most women can be either good wives or good mothers—only a fortunate few can be both." She patted my knee absently. "I like to think that if you had a chance—if your Rafe had not disappeared—you could have been one of those fortunate few." She straightened her shoulders and leaned back in the bench. "I was the good wife—a devoted, loving wife to your father. He was my everything—the very reason for my being."

She paused for a moment to gain control of her emotions. "We've never talked about these things before, Paisley. If it makes you uncomfortable...?"

I sat up quickly and took her hands in mine. Her slender fingers were cold. I warmed them for a moment in my clasp. "Mother, I'm fine. But you don't have to...."

"But I do, you see. You should know how I feel, and besides," she added with a faintly ironic little smile, "I'm rehearsing."

I bit my lip to keep from saying anything, but I knew what was coming.

"When your father and I were young I always thought that the moment one of us died the other's heart would cease to beat as well. I couldn't imagine either of us having a reason to breathe without the other. We were so very much in love, and our love only grew stronger as the years passed. It was a storybook romance, Paisley," she said with a tone of wonder in her voice. "The perfect love—I was so blessed to have that in my life."

The light of the fading afternoon glistened on the single tear that rolled down her cheek. "Horatio is my best friend. He has been my best friend since we were three years old. But when I die, I want nothing more than to spend eternity in up in Cedar Hill cemetery next to John Sterling. So you see, it simply would not be fair to marry Horatio. How can I marry a man—how can I share his bed and not his grave?"

I couldn't help it. God forgive me, I started laughing. "You mean," I sputtered, "you mean you're turning down poor old Horatio who worships the very ground you walk upon just because you want to be planted next to Dad? Surely you two could work something out? Maybe he would agree to a little plot at your feet—sort of a *ménage à trois* with the grim reaper."

She stared at me in disbelief, anger slowly replacing the sadness in her eyes. "How could you?" she gasped. "How could you belittle my love for your father?"

"Whoa!" I said angrily as I stood and brushed the grass from my jeans. "I'm not doing anything of the sort. I've always known how you felt about Dad. Believe me, I understand better than anyone how you feel. Why in the world do think I never remarried. I may not have had that Romeo and Juliet thing going with Rafe, but it was pretty damn good while it lasted. I've just never found anyone else who compared. But, Horatio...."

"That's quite enough, Paisley! Why in the world did I try to unburden myself to you? You're much too easily amused to take anything seriously!"

She flounced out of my moon garden, angrily slapping aside the trailing jasmine and leaving a hint of its bruised fragrance in her wake.

I stood there for a moment and watched her retreating back as I tried to decide whether or not to follow and continue our argument. I settled for a parting shot. "Why don't you admit the truth?" I shouted. "You're just plain chicken!"

I sat angrily on the cold metal bench, bruising my tailbone and worsening my mood. I was mad at Mother, but mostly I was mad at myself. She was merely being a silly goose. I was an insufferable brat. I should have forgiven her propensity to be a bit maudlin and then gentled her into seeing the error of her ways. Instead, all I had succeeded in doing was to make absolutely certain that she and Horatio would never have a happy ending.

"Damn!"

"Way to go, Mom."

"You heard?"

"Couldn't help but hear. I was taking a nap in the guest room and the windows were open."

"You planned it! You little imp! You know what they say about eavesdropping—someday you'll hear something you don't want to."

She laughed and set a tray of sandwiches and drinks between us on the bench. "Peace offering?"

"Sure. Why not," I sighed. "I can't afford to piss anybody else off."

"She'll get over it."

"I don't think so."

"You don't think she'll change her mind?"

I shook my head and finished chewing. "I probably made sure of that myself." I lifted up a corner of my bread and peeked cautiously inside. "What *is* this stuff?"

"Smoked tofu. Isn't it delicious?"

"No!" I put down the sandwich and turned to face my daughter. "How could I have been so stupid, Cassie?"

"You do have a knack for it, Mom."

"Gee, thanks a lot. I feel much better."

"You're not supposed to feel better. You really hurt Gran's feelings."

I felt myself getting irritated again. "She's made a mausoleum of your grandfather's memory. She can't keep living in the past."

"That's not for you to say."

"How come you're so smart, Miss Know-It-All?"

"I listen to other people conversations. More tofu?"

"Ugh!"

"Not to change the subject—but I'm dying to know. What did Horatio say to make you think Beth Davis had an accomplice?"

I ran my fingers through my hair and tried to shake off the anger and sadness I had felt since my conversation with Mother. "I told you that same night," I sighed.

"Refresh my memory."

It had gotten dark while we talked. A big peach-colored moon drifted slowly up from the horizon to cast a golden reflection in my gazing ball and at that moment I realized my garden was perfect. It was everything I had hoped for and dreamed of—full of beauty, fragrance and peace. And I was miserable.

"Mom? Horatio, remember?"

"Yeah, well...a new voice...he said her blackmail letters had changed."

"Changed? How?"

"Money for one thing. She started asking for money, and he didn't say this exactly, but I got the idea that she was making nasty threats. And Bruce said something about video tapes...."

"Bruce? What's he got to do with this?"

"Well, just damn! I can't be trusted to do anything right. Bruce will never confide in me again. I wasn't supposed to tell anyone that, but I guess you won't let it go. Correct?"

She nodded vigorously.

I was thoroughly disgusted with myself, but I knew Cassie would hound me until I told all. I sounded tired and dispirited even to myself as I told her.

"Beth threatened to show an incriminating video tape to the wife of one of Bruce's clients. The tape was made in her fancy purple *boudoir*."

"Wow! That really doesn't sound like Beth. No wonder Horatio thinks someone else in on this. What do we do next, Mom?"

"What do you mean 'we'? This whole thing has taken a nasty turn, Cassie. I don't think there should be any more 'we' involved in this. If I keep looking for Beth, it's going to be on my lonesome."

She stood up and threw the rest of her sandwich on the tray. "You always do this, Mom! You get me all excited and worked up about something and then just when it starts to get interesting, you pull the plug! How much longer do you think you can control me with this 'mother knows best' routine? I'm an adult now, you know!"

And once again I was alone with nothing but the stars and the crickets for company.

"Stupid moon garden!"

CHAPTER EIGHTEEN

I had a ridiculous dream that night. Horatio and Mother danced madly around my moon garden on stilts. They were wearing elegant evening clothes topped off with elaborate headgear made of feathers and sequins. When the big clock on the courthouse struck midnight, Horatio threw their hats into the air. As they floated back to the ground I could see the hats were really scanties from Lady Valentines. I tried to pick one up but Aggie swooped in and grabbed it out of my hands. She went running back down the lane with me hot on her heels, screaming for Cassie to come and help me.

"Mom! Mom! Wake up!"

Cassie pounded on my pillow and shook me.

"What's...?"

"You had another bad dream. You were screaming for me at the top of your lungs!"

"Aggie," I mumbled. "Aggie has the panties."

"Oh, for goodness sakes! You're beginning to worry me, Mom. What's wrong with you? These dreams are getting out of hand."

I struggled upright in bed and turned on my bedside lamp. The light blinded us both for a minute, but not before I saw that Cassie was still fully dressed.

"Hey, what's up with you? You going somewhere?"

She turned away so that I wouldn't see her face and mumbled, "Maybe. What's it to ya?"

Anger prickled the hairs on the back of my neck. "Now, see here, Missy! That borders on...."

Cassie sighed and fell heavily back on the bed, "Rats!"

Aggie heard her and yelped from somewhere behind closed doors.

"What is going on, Cassie? Why do you have Aggie locked up? Not that it isn't a good idea."

She raised up on one elbow to face me. "It's all your fault, you know."

"Well, I'm sure of that."

"You wouldn't let me help. So I was going to find Beth on my own and show you I was good for something after all."

I suspected the little catch in her voice was a theatrical touch, but nevertheless, she made her point. I felt like a heel.

"I'm just trying to...."

"I know, I know! You're trying to protect me! And you should! I know you love me, Mom; but if you trusted me you'd give me some space."

"Cassie, that line didn't work when you were seventeen. Haven't you had a creative thought since then?"

She bounced up on the bed and crossed her legs Indian style. Her brown eyes sparkled and her voice was full of excitement. "You bet I have! Trade?"

"Trade what?" I asked, with a chuckle.

"Let me be your 'really truly sidekick' with no holds barred. Promise me you won't say, 'I'm afraid this is too dangerous for you, Cassie,' even once, and I'll tell you."

"Tell me what"

"Promise?"

We had been down this road many times. I loved my daughter more than she could even guess, but she was right. It was time for me to let her have some space. I tried to comfort myself with the knowledge that the space she wanted was by my side instead of somewhere in sub-Saharan Africa with the Peace Corps, or in a cheap third floor walk-up in New York City with a hairy wanna-be actor.

"Promise." The catch in my own throat was genuine. "Now, go let Aggie out and fix us some hot chocolate. I'll meet you in the library after I splash some water on my face."

"Super! Thanks, Mom! You're the best!"

When she was gone I blew my nose on a tissue from the box Mother kept placing by the side of my bed no matter how many times I removed it. I knew why she put it there and it made me mad to think she would believe that I still blew my nose on the sheets like I did when I was a child. I carried the box with me to the bathroom and left it there after I washed my face and brushed my hair back in a tangled ponytail.

I glanced in the mirror, hoping I wouldn't see a woman old enough to have a twenty-three year old daughter, but son-of-a-gun, there she was—great cheekbones, maybe, and eyes still green and bright, but the tiniest of lines were gathering at the corners in readiness for the battle to come—the battle between time and me—the one I wouldn't win.

I slipped into a cozy robe and house slippers, and shuffled into the library. Cassie already had the hot chocolate and a plate of buttered toast waiting on the low table between the two red chintz sofas.

"Ummm, this is yummy, Cassie. Thanks."

"Sorry about before, Mom. I probably wouldn't have really sneaked out of the house. I was just considering it real hard."

"I know."

"But you won't take back your promise, will you?"

"Have I ever taken back a promise?"

She wiped chocolate and marshmallow off her mouth with one of Mother's linen napkins and grinned back. "Just the one about the pony."

I laughed. "Don't go there, girlfriend." I set my cup down on the tray and grabbed another toast corner. "Now how about your part of the bargain—what's your great idea?"

"Interviews!"

The delight in her voice made me smile, but at three o'clock in the morning what she said made no sense at all. "Pardon?"

"The morning that Beth Davis came out here to see you she was talking to Gran about a series of interviews she had written for the newspaper last year. It was called, 'A Modest Collection of Recollections'."

"Sounds like our Beth, all right," I sneered.

"Don't be mean, Mom." She stuck her finger in the foamy residue of marshmallow on the inside of her cup and sucked the sweetness thoughtfully. "The interesting part is that she interviewed all kinds of people: a banker, a minister, a farmer, a basketball player, even an eighty-year-old woman who used to be an exotic dancer."

I yawned. I was tired of Bethlehem Davis. She had been more trouble than she was worth.

"And?"

"And, well...I think we should read those articles. We might find a clue."

The next morning I reluctantly followed my daughter to the Whitherspoon Public Library. When we were told that an accident involving a water pipe and a carpenter's errant drill had caused a flood in the basement where the newspapers were, I gladly turned on my heels and prepared to leave.

"But," called the perky assistant librarian, "I'm sure the Gazette office will have every back issue in the computer, or on microfilm. My cousin works there. I'll call him and tell him you're coming. Just ask for 'Mike'."

"Mike" turned out to be a grumpy ex-typesetter on the mean side of sixty. Except for the few thin wisps of faded brown that stuck up at odd angles over his large ears and forehead, he was almost bald. His eyes were sharp and quick behind narrow steel rimmed glasses, and the nicotine stains on his fingers and caffeine stains on his teeth confirmed his nervous habits.

"Dang computers!" he complained vehemently. "Can't ever get 'em to work right!" He gave the hapless monitor on the front desk a resounding thump with his fist. "Gladys! Come out here and fix this dang thing! The picture went all dark again."

A tidy little woman with a worried look on her otherwise pleasant face came at a half trot from some inner office. "Michael, if you've broken another...! Excuse me, ladies," she apologized. "I didn't know anyone was here." She gently pulled Mike to one side and fiddled with the computer for a moment. "You're lucky!" she said with a relieved smile. "It'll just have to reboot."

"Well, these gals want some back issues of the paper. Should I take them down to the morgue?"

"Yes, if you please, Michael. Take the 'ladies' down to the 'archives.' I'd do it myself but I'm...."

"Then do it yourself. I'm goin' on a break."

The little woman sighed with exasperation as Mike stormed out pulling a bag of Red Dog chew from his back pocket. "You'll have to excuse Michael," she said. "Ever since we computerized he's been feeling like a fifth wheel. Typesetting was the only job he ever knew. I wish he would go ahead and retire, but he loves the newspaper. Has more facts in his stubborn old head than anyone in Rowan Springs. He's a walking encyclopedia and nobody cares." She smiled. "Well, maybe me. I care; but then we've been married for forty years."

Gladys led us to a back staircase that was steeper than I liked, and descended with the agility of a mountain goat. After flipping on a bank of overhead florescent lights, she pointed out a row of file cabinets against one wall of the stuffy basement room.

"You'll probably find whatever you're looking for in those files," she said. "Help yourself to the table and chairs, ladies. Just, please remember to put things back in the right drawers."

By design we had been vague about our exact mission so when Gladys hurried back upstairs we looked at each other in consternation.

"Where do we start, Mom?"

"I haven't the faintest idea, kiddo. This is your show. I'm just along for the ride."

She got lucky with the third drawer. "Here it is! 'Bethlehem Davis—Recollections, notes and background'!"

"I bet you couldn't do that again!"

"Why not?" she laughed. "Leonard could!"

I decided to read the interviews first. That way, I reasoned, the notes would make more sense. By the time I finished with the fifth one, I was bored, hungry, and certain of my initial opinion of Beth's writing. "Holy cow! What a hack! She should be legally denied the use of the alphabet! I can't take this anymore, Cassie. Can't we take a break for lunch, or dinner, or a European vacation?"

She looked up from a manila folder her nose had been buried in. There was an ink smudge on her cheek and her crisp white blouse wasn't either anymore.

"But what about my idea, Mom? We can't just give up," she pleaded. "Not now, not until we've read them all."

I sank back down in my hard wooden chair feeling trapped and resentful. At that moment I didn't care if Beth had been kidnapped by a Voodoo witch doctor who wanted to turn her into a zombie. I looked around in desperation, hoping to find a way out. That's when I saw the copier.

"Copies!" I shouted happily.

"What?" she sniffed.

"Let's make copies and take them home where we can read them at our leisure."

The dark cloud began to lift from her pretty face. "If you promise you'll really read them and not just get all leisurely on me.

"Look, Cassie, you've sneezed fourteen times in the past hour. Your eyes are red and watery from all this dust and you're filthy dirty. Not to mention the fact that I'm starving. It just makes sense."

"Okay," she decided quickly. "I'll pull the files and you copy."

Copies turned out to be ten cents a page. Gladys collected twenty-two dollars and forty cents from me and said, "Ya'll come back, now. And if you see Michael outside anywhere, tell him I want him to run an errand for me."

CHAPTER NINETEEN

Reading Beth's interviews was like looking at a gallery of unfinished portraits. She had an uncanny ability to gloss over the important things and dwell on trivial facts which left the reader with a "so what" feeling. She also had an obsession with other people's pets. According to her articles, the mayor had a French poodle, the loan officer at the bank adored his ten-year-old boa constrictor, and the three hundred pound high school basketball coach was the proud owner of a Chihuahua puppy. I wasn't surprised to see that her interview with me touched only briefly on my writing career and focused primarily on the "darling antics of Paisley's captivating canine as she cavorted through the calla lilies in Anna Howard Sterling's charming floricultural landscape."

"Oh, for pity's sake!" I groaned.

"Mom," warned Cassie, "you promised!"

"And you promised me food," I complained. "Isn't that chili ready yet?" The raw vegetable tray Cassie had fixed for lunch was long gone, and the mouth-watering smell of cumin and oregano was driving me crazy. It had rained steadily all afternoon, and the air was damp and cold—a perfect night for chili, even if it was vegetarian.

"Ummm," she said absently. "I'll go check in a minute. I'm right in the middle of something that might be interesting."

"Cassie!"

"Oh, all right! But don't touch my stuff. Bowl or cup?"

"Are you kidding? Bowl! Big bowl! And lots of oyster crackers, please."

"You mean polenta. Crackers are bad for you. They turn into a gooey white paste in your small...."

"Please," I begged. "Spare me the gruesome details."

As soon as she left the room, I stood and stretched. My back and shoulders ached from sitting too long in one position. Then, intrigued by the "oohs" and "aahs" I had been hearing from Cassie all afternoon, I took her place on the other sofa and looked over the papers she was reading, careful not to disturb anything.

At first glance I didn't see anything other than the same sort of drivel I had been subjected to, but then my sleeve caught on the edge of a folder and spilled its more interesting contents out onto the floor.

"Damn!"

"I asked you not to touch my stuff." Cassie set the heavy tray of food on the hearthside and knelt down to retrieve her papers. We had a short tug-of-war but I managed to keep possession of the one I was reading.

"Why didn't you tell me about Beth's interview with 'Prison Inmate No.1898A'?" I asked. "Were you saving it for dessert?"

She busied herself with our dinner—setting the bowls of steaming hot chili topped with triangles of polenta and a sprig of cilantro on placemats to protect Mother's table.

"Seriously, Cassie, why didn't you mention this before? You could have saved us a lot of time."

She sank down on the sofa, a pleased little smile on her face. "You really think it's important?"

"Well, yeah!"

"I was afraid you would laugh at me for pointing out the obvious."

"Nonsense! You were saving it for the moment when I threw my hands in the air and gave up."

"Guilty," she laughed. "Eat your chili while it's hot."

We discussed the value of Cassie's find throughout dinner. Her main concern was that I might settle on our convicted felon and overlook someone equally, or even more important.

"It's for sure he couldn't have had anything to do with Beth's disappearance," she insisted. "He's in the poky."

"Maybe, maybe not."

Now it was her turn to groan. "I love it when you so noncommittal, Mom. What do you mean by that?"

"Well, you're right that he couldn't have abducted Beth

himself, but maybe he belongs to some nefarious criminal gang with long arms that stretch...."

"You're beginning to sound like Beth."

I threw the papers on the table. "That's it! I'm done."

Cassie ignored me. "I suppose he could have arranged for her disappearance, but somehow he doesn't look like the 'crime boss type'."

"There's a picture?"

She fished around in several folders and came up with a wallet-sized black and white snapshot of #1898A: a thin-faced and obviously unhappy young man who stared defiantly at the camera while he held a plaque against his chest bearing his new name and destination.

"Looks like he wasn't too thrilled about going to Teddyville," I observed. "But you're right. He doesn't seem experienced enough to run a crime family. Of course, according to this date, he's been under lock and key for almost six years. He could have learned a lot in jail. I wish we had a more recent photograph. What's his real name?"

"I don't know. There's nothing with his name on it anywhere in Beth's interview. She just refers to him as 'Number 1898'."

"'A'," I reminded her. "Don't forget the 'A'."

"Maybe we could call the prison and find out who he is."

"Let's do what you said and comb through the rest of these interviews first. As much as I hate to keep reading this crap, you're right about making sure we don't jump to conclusions and overlook something."

Cassie got up and went to the double French doors. "Did you hear a car?" she asked, peering out into the wet, gloomy night.

"Horatio, maybe?"

"I don't see anything. And I got the idea from Gran this morning that Horatio won't be coming around much anymore." She looked at me accusingly. There was deep regret and sorrow in her eyes.

I sank back in the down sofa cushions seeking their comforting embrace.

"I know," I sighed. "I screwed things up big time."

"What are you going to do about it?"

Her voice had the trusting tone of a little girl whose parent still has the power to fix the bike, patch the dress, and soothe the pain of a scraped knee.

"I'm not so sure I can make it better, Cassie."

"You'll think of something," she said confidently. "You always do. Dessert?"

"Absolutely! Wha'cha got?"

"Non-fat vanilla yogurt."

The yogurt wasn't so bad, especially with the fat slice of juicy ripe mango on top. But the rest of the night was a bust. We spent three tedious hours going over and over each of the twenty interviews and found nothing else that raised our suspicions.

"I think '1898A' is our man," I finally decided. "The rest of these people are just too boring to be bad. God, how do they get up in the morning and face such monotonous days?"

Cassie yawned. "A lot of people find comfort in tedium, Mom. Not many adventurers anymore. I guess all the pirate kings died out with your Mr. Clark 'Grable'."

"Time to go to bed, Cassie," I laughed. "Leave the dishes. I'll wash up."

Cassie had been very economical in the kitchen. One pot and two bowls later I was done. I hesitated a moment at the door of Mother's bedroom before I left that side of the house, but when I didn't hear a sound or see any light in her dressing room, I decided to wait until tomorrow before making a fool of myself again.

The rain was still falling in a steady rhythm against the roof. I slipped on some pajamas and crawled under the covers in anticipation of a cozy night, but two hours later I was still staring at the hazy outline of the ceiling fan in the darkness above me.

I had made a lot of mistakes in my life—said many things better left unsaid, but this time I had topped them all. I had hurt my mother deeply, and although he didn't know it—for I'm sure she didn't tell him what I'd done—I had destroyed Horatio's only chance for happiness. Horatio was my best friend, too. It was something I had never realized before, but it was true. I relied on him—his knowledge, his experience, and his wisdom. And I enjoyed his company more than any other's despite the thirty years between us. I truly wanted him to marry Mother and be an official member of our family. So why had I opened my big mouth and spoiled it all?

Was I selfishly concerned that Horatio would take something away from me—take my place in this house? Change the group dynamic so that I was less important, less loved? I lay there and did some deep soul-searching while it rained.

The rain stopped shortly before dawn when I finally fell asleep on pillow wet with tears and a heart heavier than ever. All I had discovered was that I didn't know myself as well as I had thought.

Around ten the next morning I stumbled into the kitchen, bleary-eyed and dry-mouthed. Mother was standing at the sink so I gave up on a glass of water and opened the refrigerator to see what else I could find to quench my thirst. I'll swear to my dying day that I never laid a finger on that egg carton, so how a dozen eggs ended up splashed all over the floor I'll never know. Mother flashed "thoroughly disapproving look number two" in my direction, lifted the hem of her dressing gown and swept imperiously out of the kitchen without a word.

I grabbed the orange juice carton and defiantly drank directly from the mouth. Most of the juice spilled on my pajamas but I got enough down to give me the energy to clean up all the mess. Half a roll of paper towels later, I knocked on Mother's dressing room door.

"Whoever it is," she called, "go away. I want to be alone."

Knowing that most people who say they want to be alone really just want attention, I opened the door and stepped inside. Mother was propped up in her ivory damask chaise reading a book. The glasses she hardly ever used were perched on the end of her nose. She looked at me over the thin gold frames as though I were a bug.

"I haven't seen you in a couple of days," I mumbled. "I just wanted to make sure you were okay."

"Well," she demanded angrily, "are you satisfied?"

"Mother, don't you think it's time to call a truce? I'm really sorry. Won't you forgive me?"

"Why should I?"

"I can't think of a reason, other than I love you and Cassie—and Horatio—more than anything else on this earth and I want us to all live together and be happy," I pleaded humbly.

She took off her glasses and put down her book. She made me wait a long time for her answer. I stood there holding my breath.

"Paisley, this isn't about a broken teacup. Or a dozen wasted eggs, although I do wish you would be more careful. Horatio Raleigh is a fine man. He deserves to be treated with the utmost in dignity and respect. I'm sure you'll agree with that?"

I nodded my head like a parrot, hopeful that she was on the right track, the one I was praying for. "Absolutely, that's why...."

She held her hand up and I shut up.

"He wants to marry me. I cannot marry him." Her hand wilted and fell gracefully back to the book in her lap. "It's unfair to accept his attentions and allow him to keep hoping I'll change my mind. I care far too much about him—respect him too much to use him that way."

I opened my mouth, but she stopped me again.

"You had your chance, too, Paisley. Last year a good man was in love with you, and I think you loved him. Yet you wouldn't marry him, either. So you see, you're really not so different from me.

"There's one big difference between us, Mother."

"What?" she asked skeptically.

"You know where your husband is."

She took a deep ragged breath and picked up her book again.

"Paisley, you have said quite enough about things that are really none of your affair. I would greatly appreciate it if you would say no more."

"But...."

"Enough!"

And she waved me angrily out of the room.

CHAPTER TWENTY

I dragged my sorry self into the shower and emerged feeling only slightly less rotten. I didn't even fuss at Aggie when she took up residence on my down pillow. In my woeful frame of mind, I didn't want to be responsible for depriving anyone else of their heart's desire.

The new lavender silk blouse in my closet shamed me even more. I chose a blue chambray shirt instead, and slipped on a linen jacket because I wanted to go to town. I wanted to see Cassie. My daughter could nearly always jolly me out of a bad mood. But this time I knew she'd be far from sympathetic. I was supposed to have fixed things with Mother, not make them worse. So, when I got to the end of the driveway, instead of turning towards town I headed out to the country with Watson's windows down and my hair blowing wildly in the morning breeze.

The fields of soybeans, sorghum, and tobacco were growing like crazy. Kitchen gardens in back of farmhouses were thriving as well. Small boys with handmade signs sold the excess of their bounty at vegetable stands on the sides of country lanes. Most of them smiled and waved when I passed them without stopping, but when one mooned me as I drove on, I had to laugh. After a while, I began to relax and enjoy the ride.

I drove for over an hour, meandering over narrow roads with one lane bridges, and finally over a dirt track to the bird sanctuary at the beginning of the "creek" part of Teddy Creek. It was there in the reeds and marshes where the osprey and wild ducks nested that the stream was born—where it began its journey—before it grew in size and force and emptied into the Cumberland River at the site of the prison by the same name.

I sat and watched the birds for over an hour. I would have

stayed longer, but I was hungry and it was long after noon. Regretfully, I whispered goodbye to the family of ducklings I had been spying on, and turned to back in the direction of the main road. I felt much better. In my reverie, I had formulated a plan of sorts.

I passed an orchard on my way into town and impulsively stopped for a basket of fresh peaches and a sack of "peach leather." I had almost finished the rich, chewy strips of the dried fruit by the time I pulled up in front of Bruce Hawkins' law office.

The pretty blonde who was acting as his temporary receptionist told me Bruce's aunt was on vacation in New Zealand. She offered me a cup of really good coffee while she regaled me with anecdotes about the transfer of powers.

"You wouldn't believe it," she giggled. "It was like handing over the keys to Buckingham Palace! And I swear, I still can't open all the files. I know the old..., er, she held out on me." Her pretty smile soured and turned into an unattractive pout. "How's a gal supposed to do her job without the proper equipment?"

I thought the sudden arching of back and thrust of bosom was an answer to her own rhetorical question until I realized another client had quietly entered the office. I watched as Blondie swing her hips in the man's direction and offer him the same cup of coffee but with lots more sugar.

Bruce turned bright red when he poked his head out to ask for the next client and saw me. He ushered me inside with a stammered apology.

"Paisley, eh...well, when my aunt...."

"Don't bother, Bruce," I teased. "She's probably your niece, or something."

"But she is!"

"You're kidding!"

He laughed and motioned for me to take a seat in the chair opposite his desk.

"Megan Flaherty. She's Mary's sister's youngest. She's on, er...hiatus from college."

"Dropped out?"

"Yeah," he admitted with a big grin. "Tremendous loss to Fraternity Row, I imagine."

"How is Mary?"

"Fine, Paisley—wonderful in fact." His grin extended almost to his ears. "We found a house," he announced proudly. "The nursery is this color," he said pointing to a robin's egg blue paint spot on his wrist.

"A boy! Congratulations, Bruce."

He was still blushing with pride when he asked, "What can I do for you today?"

I stood and walked over to the window wondering how I should frame the question. Finally, I decided to speak plainly. I turned to face him.

"Tell me the names of your clients—the ones Beth Davis was blackmailing."

Bruce looked truly astonished, then pained, and finally relieved. "You're joking, right? Paisley, you're really a trip!"

"I'm not joking, Bruce," I assured him.

"But...."

I sighed dramatically and flopped back down in my chair.

"I know. And stop looking like I stole your kid's bike."

"How did you...?"

I laughed. "Elementary, my dear! Your first child—and a boy—give me a break! I wouldn't be surprised if you haven't already started on a tree house."

"I ordered the plans last week," he said with a sheepish grin. "Two stories—with a swing and a sliding board."

I sat on the edge of my chair and clasped my hands in front of me on his desk. I tried my best to look earnest and entirely without guile.

"Okay, Bruce, I'm impressed with your ethics, and your fatherly instincts—and I accept the fact that you cannot divulge any privileged information." I sighed heavily once again. "I'll just have to find out some other way."

I pretended to shrug away my disappointment and go on to another subject. "So maybe you can do something else for me."

"Name it, Paisley," he said, obviously relieved that I had not forced the issue.

Right on cue, I popped the real question. "Get me inside Teddyville, can you? I want to interview a prisoner."

He watched me over tented fingers for a few seconds before he answered. "Whatever for?"

"A book, of course," I lied. "And Cassie wants to go, too."

"You're crazy," he sputtered. "Do you know what those men would do if they saw her?" He took off his glasses and rubbed the spot between his eyes. "You don't know what you're asking, Paisley. Teddyville is a maximum security prison. Those guys are the worst of the worst."

"All of them?" I asked, remembering Nell Jane's father.

"If they didn't deserve it when they went in, they did something on the inside to deserve full-fledged membership. I beg you to reconsider going yourself, Paisley, but I absolutely refuse to facilitate your taking Cassie."

"Then you tell her. She won't believe me."

I got up from the chair and tried to look glum—tried not to gloat about my victory until I was safely out of his office. For a smart man, I thought, Bruce Hawkins was easy to bamboozle

The over night rain had not done much for the streets of Rowan Springs. Leaves and other debris clogged the manhole covers and grates, and many of the roads were full of standing water. The honeycomb of limestone caves that lay beneath the town always filled up quickly with a heavy downpour, and there was nowhere for the gutters to drain.

I picked my way across Main Street, carefully avoiding the biggest puddles. I had almost made it to the other side when a pick up truck splashed dirty water all over my jeans. I gave the driver a dirty look as he stared at me in his rearview mirror. I started to give him a three-fingered salute, but there was something about the man's face—something sinister that made me shudder and hurry on into the warmth and comfort of the coffee shop.

Cassie was busy with a book order so Mindy whipped up my "super espresso latte whachmacallit." When she was finished, she plopped a cherry on top and handed me a chocolate-coated peppermint candy spoon to stir it with.

"Special of the day, Miz DeLeon," she chirped. "Isn't it just the yummiest?"

After several weeks of Cassie's restrictions on my diet, I thought I would be eager to gobble up the mountain of whipped cream and slurp down the chocolate; but instead, I found myself looking in dismay at the fat grams and empty calories. All I really wanted was a nice hot cup of Earl Grey with lemon.

I smiled weakly back at her and nibbled on the cherry. I didn't want to hurt the girl's feelings, and most of all I didn't want to mention the word "diet."

"Sorry, Mindy," said Cassie as she swooped in and grabbed the coffee. "Mom's watching her...."

"Just some hot tea, please," I interrupted. "If you don't mind." And then to change the subject, "Seen any aliens lately, Mindy?"

"Oh, not you, too, Miz DeLeon," she cried mournfully. Everybody in town is teasing me about that one. I wish I'd never talked to that old witc...woman. Everybody's making fun of her, too. She's still claiming to see things."

The tiny little hairs on my forearms were standing at attention. "What kind of things?"

"Demons, black-hooded devils, the usual stuff. But nobody takes her seriously any more. The girls at '9-1-1' won't even take her calls."

Cassie had swept off the patio and dried the benches earlier. She led me out to my favorite spot under to the Japanese maple and sat down next to me.

"What were you doing in Bruce's office, Mom? Wow! Isn't that niece of Mary's something? Half the men in town have been in there for one thing or another this week. Poor Bruce should get a revolving door." She laughed. "Or maybe sell tickets!" She laughed even harder.

"You still want to know why I was there?" I asked irritably. I didn't want to miss this opportunity. I was hoping she, or Mindy would have seen me go inside. I was counting on it.

"Yeah, sure," she said, wiping laughter tears from her eyes. "But first, I want to tell you I've changed my mind about going to jail with you—if you don't mind, that is." She grabbed my hand and held it tight. "Of course, I'll go if you really need me, Mom," she offered sincerely. "But if you don't care, I'd just as soon wait outside. Too many bad vibes in there for me. Now, what were you doing at Bruce's office?"

"Uh, well...I wanted to congratulate him. The baby and all," I finished lamely, somewhat miffed that she had stolen my thunder.

She looked at me speculatively. "When did you find out? Mindy and I just learned it this morning when he came over for a bagel and coffee. He said they hadn't told anyone yet."

I searched my feeble brain and came up with nothing. Finally I turned over my teacup instead of answering.

"Oh, damn! I am so sorry, Cassie."

Mother was still barricaded inside her rooms so I took Aggie out for a short walk and then headed for the library. It had been ages since I spent time with Leonard and the outline for our new book. My agent would be calling sometime soon to inquire about my progress. I had to get to work. I didn't need any more guilt.

I turned on the laptop and waited for all the gizmos to warm up while I tried to remember where we had left off—something about the Columbian drug cartel and a venomous snake.

My mind wandered as I looked out the French doors at the familiar scene. The sun had come out to dry up all the puddles and the backyard had a fresh, scrubbed-clean look. New leaves were sprouting on the climbing rose Mother had asked me to plant next to the carriage house. I reminded myself to spray for aphids sometime this week.

I was wondering how long it would be before I heard from Bruce about my trip to Teddyville when the phone rang.

"Paisley," he said, "is tomorrow afternoon at two o'clock okay for you?"

CHAPTER TWENTY-ONE

Cassie drove around the prison parking lot twice before she decided where the best vantage point was.

"I can see the front gate better from here," she announced when she finally picked her spot. "The side lot's too far away and I wouldn't be able to see you coming out. This is perfect—and it's right by the river with nothing to obstruct the view."

She pulled into the one vacant space in the narrow parking strip across the street from Teddyville Prison and turned off the engine. The wild waters of the Cumberland River raced by not ten feet from the Watson's front bumper.

We sat still for a minute and watched, awed by the power of the raging waters.

"Ugh," said Cassie with a grimace. "It's dirty, and there aren't any boats."

She was right. The water was the color of the mud on the banks—the color of the earth over which it flowed. An occasional small sapling bobbed along in the current, but except for that frantic bit of greenery caught in the current there was nothing to see in that half-mile wide avenue of swiftly moving reddish-brown water.

"Can anybody even drive a boat in that?"

"Pilot, Cassie, pilot—or steer. I'm not sure which, myself. Barges, probably—coal barges," I guessed, wishing I knew more. "But I had no idea the current was so strong!"

"Ugh," Cassie repeated with a shudder, "me neither."

I got out of Watson, trying not to look at the dark gray towers and barbed wire that stretched over the expanse of a block or more down the riverfront. I bent down to check my lipstick in the side mirror and was surprised to see how pale and anxious I looked. Shaking off the feeling of dread, I tucked in my shirt and brushed off my jacket before I turned back to gaze up at the imposing stone edifice in front of me.

Rough-hewn stone walls loomed up so high that I got a crick in my neck trying to see the top. Pale greenish lichen coated the stones so that they resembled those of the ancient ruins I had seen in Europe. No wonder, I thought, that they call this "the Castle on the Cumberland." That's what it looked like, the castle of an unforgiving and tyrannical king, complete with the towers where he imprisoned his most disloyal subjects.

Above those towers, the sky was clear and blue, with just the tiniest wisps of white. There were few, if any, birds flying in that azure sky—as if they were too tactful, too diplomatic to flaunt their freedom in front of the men trapped behind those forbidding stone walls.

"You sure you're okay?" asked Cassie. "I can change my mind and go in with you if you want."

"No," I assured her hastily. "I'm fine. And I won't be long. Bruce set everything up with the warden. 'Inmate #1898A' will be ready and waiting for me in fifteen minutes. I have just enough time to sign in and get frisked, or whatever they do here."

I tried not to look at my daughter. Cassie had an uncanny ability to read my face, and I had always had a hard time hiding my emotions.

"Scared, Mom?"

"Of course not! It's just that I haven't ever been inside Frankenstein's castle before." I laughed and turned to face her for the truth. "Well, yes, maybe a little," I admitted. "But mostly I'm afraid I'll say the wrong thing—screw it all up. I'm really going in kind of blind, you know. We don't have much to go on. I'll have to bluff a lot if I want to find out anything that might tell us where Beth is—if he even knows."

"You'll do just fine," she promised. "You've had years of training with Leonard."

"You're right, pumpkin." I smiled and kissed her on the cheek.

I turned to wave after I crossed the street and climbed the steps to the front gate, but all I saw was Cassie's back as she shivered and got back in the car and out of the wind.

Teddyville Prison ceased to look like a medieval castle as

soon as I entered the big front doors. The vestibule and front hall were wide and ugly and painted a depressing institutional green. Long wooden benches lined the plain plaster walls and the floor was a dark gray concrete that had been polished to an onyx shine.

The heels of my new loafers sounded like castanets as they clicked on the floor in the empty hallway. I walked almost all the way to the end before I saw another living soul.

"Name, please?" boomed the guard who appeared from nowhere.

"Wow!" I gasped, "Paisley, Paisley Sterling. Geez, you nearly scared me to death!"

"Identification?" he repeated without even acknowledging my remarks.

I fished around in my bag and came up with my driver's license.

"Says here you're Paisley DeLeon. Make up your mind, lady. Which one are you?"

I tried smiling but my lips refused to cooperate. "Both," I stammered. "I mean—I'm a writer. I use my maiden name when I have my writing cap on." I tried to smile again when I realized how juvenile and silly that sounded.

"Well, take your cap off in here, lady." He wrote out "DELEON" in big block letters on a pass and shoved it in my hand. "And do what you're told. If you don't—you could get somebody killed—probably yourself."

He pointed to the window at the end of the corridor. "Go down there and tell the guard who you want to see."

"I think my lawyer...," I began foolishly.

He grabbed my shoulders, turned me around, and gave me a little push in the right direction. "Do as you're told!"

I clamped my jaw down so hard my teeth hurt as I fought my rising temper. I wanted to tell him where to get off in the worst way. Only the thought of the explanation I would have to give Cassie made me march, as ordered, down the hall and knock on the window. Still fuming, I probably knocked a little too hard.

"Hey, hey, hey! Take it easy. I'll be there as soon as I can."

I heard the voice but I had to wait another five minutes before I saw the man. This guard wasn't a 'lean, mean, fightin' machine' like "Big Bad Dude" down the hall—in fact he was short and fat and bald, with a Bugs Bunny overbite and an open Twinkie package shoved in his breast pocket. He wiped pastry cream from his lips with the back of a pudgy hand and waddled over to the desk where he paused deliberately—taking the time to adjust his ample behind comfortably in the chair before he addressed me.

"Now, have we calmed down a bit, sister? Ready to tell us who you want to see without raising a ruckus?"

I closed my eyes and counted to ten. Telling him I wasn't his sister, and that I WAS CALM wouldn't get me anywhere. I was beginning to get the picture. The way to get what you wanted in prison was to appear humble and cooperative.

"Yes, sir," I said with my most winning smile. "And I didn't mean to raise a ruckus."

"You calling me a liar?" he growled.

I decided not to answer. The anger in my voice might give me away. Instead I shook my head and lowered my eyes.

"That's more like it! Now, who you here for? I haven't seen you before, and we haven't gotten a new shipment lately. Must be an old-timer."

"Number 1898A", I said as softly as I could. I was afraid to mention my lawyer again, but the guard must have remembered something because he searched through the mess on his desk and came up with the letter Bruce had faxed to the warden.

"You Paisley DeLeon?"

"Yes."

"My, my, my! 'Baby' Jake Bradley has quite a little fan club!" he said with a suggestive leer.

"Jake?" I was stunned. Surely it was too much of a coincidence to expect that #1898A might be little Nell Jane's father.

"Jacob Bradley. Hey! You not trying to pull a fast one, are you? Says in this here letter you want to see him in the family room. How come you don't know his name? You really family?"

"Why...why, of course," I stammered. "It's just that we always called him Jacob. He's a distant cousin on my father's side. I haven't seen him in years. I promised Aunt Hettie...."

"Yahta, yahta, yahta," he interrupted. "Like I give a rat's ass. Sign here."

He shoved a clipboard through the slot in the window but didn't offer me a pen. I fished around in my bag and found the black Waterman Horatio had given me for my birthday. I signed the form and started to put the pen away.

"Hey! Better let me keep that," he said, as he stuck his hand through the window and grabbed it. Could be used as a weapon. Got anything else like this?"

I shook my head again, too full of anger to speak.

"Better let me check." He stuck the Waterman in his pocket next to the Twinkie and reached up through the window for my handbag.

I hated the fat slob for holding something that belonged to me, something I treasured, even for a moment. The idea of him pawing through my personal effects made me want to throw up.

"May...may I have a receipt for the pen, please," I dared, hoping to stall him for a moment while I slipped Cassie's picture into my pocket. I wasn't going to give him a chance to drool over my baby.

His round face grew red with anger but before he could think of an answer someone knocked loudly on the door behind him.

"Coming in, Roy. Check me," a man called out.

"Roy" pried himself out of the chair and shuffled over to peer through the peephole. Satisfied, he opened the door and let another guard inside. When he turned around my Waterman had disappeared. It was his word against mine that he ever had it in the first place. I was furious.

The new guard was dressed smartly in a starched uniform with a knife pleats in the trousers and shiny black shoes. He took his uniform cap off and placed it carefully on one of the other desks.

"Any problems?" he asked as he gingerly removed the Twinkie from Roy's pocket and dropped it in the garbage can.

"Now see here," Roy whined. "That was my lunch!"

The other guard ignored his protests and inclined his head towards me. "This lady been taken care of properly? Has she been cleared? Is she clean?"

Roy absently nodded his head "yes" to all the questions while he stared regretfully at the discarded Twinkie.

I knew this was the time to get my pen back—and get Roy into a mess of trouble because he had not even begun to search me; but I also knew that this new guard would give me a very thorough going over. I had nothing to hide, but at the same time, I didn't relish being manhandled. I reluctantly decided to keep my mouth shut.

The "family room" of Teddyville Prison had all the charm of a Transylvanian dungeon. The color scheme and the concrete floor—minus the polish—were the same as that of the hall. Two of the long wooden benches formed a "conversation area" in one corner and a large wooden table and six chairs occupied another.

I sat down at one of the uncomfortable straight-backed chairs and tried not to be intimidated by the big mirror on the wall that I suspected was one-way glass. I slipped my handbag behind me in the chair, hoping that no one else would take an interest in it, and tried to relax.

I didn't have to wait very long before I heard the metallic clink of handcuffs. I stood up quickly in preparation for my little performance just as Jacob Bradley pushed open the door.

"Cousin Jacob!" I cried enthusiastically. "You remember me—Cousin Paisley, Paisley Sterling DeLeon."

The man glared angrily at me for a moment and turned to leave.

"I saw Nell Jane the other day," I blurted out. "She's grown so much I hardly knew her."

Jacob Bradley paused and then turned back with a sly smile.

"Cousin Paisley," he grinned. "How very good to see you."

CHAPTER TWENTY-TWO

Jake Bradley wasn't just a handsome man—he was beautiful—angelic—with soulful brown eyes and full lips that tilted upwards with just the right amount of self-deprecation. Dressed in regulation jeans and blue denim shirt, he was tall and lean, with bones and muscles in all the right places. He could easily have been a movie star playing the role of a prisoner—with only a hint of the pimply faced teenage in the photograph.

He sat down in a chair across from me and placed his manacled wrists on the table.

"If you say this is a conjugal visit they'll take these handcuffs off," he said in a voice full of innuendo.

My cheeks burned with anger as I lowered my eyes and tried to think of a response that wouldn't make him mad enough to get up and leave.

"Don't worry, cousin," he laughed softly. "You can't blame me for trying. You're a very pretty lady."

"What about your wife?" I asked pointedly. "Doesn't she ever come to see you?"

He leaned back and balanced his chair easily on two legs while he laughed. "That cow?" he finally managed. "She's too busy entertaining half the men in Lakeland County to worry about me. Besides, she divorced me three years ago. Had the papers served on my birthday. Pretty thoughtful, huh? Especially since it's her fault I'm in here in the first place."

"Her fault?"

"Yeah." The chair legs slammed down on the floor, as his mood grew surly. I realized I had made a mistake. We didn't have much time and I had gotten the conversation off on the wrong track. I had to get him to talk about Beth somehow.

"Don't you have other visitors?"

"Like that fathead of a shrink they send around once month?"

"Well, no. I was really thinking of someone else."

"She sent you here, didn't she?" he whispered excitedly as he leaned in closer.

"She who?" I prompted.

"You know who! Stop kidding around, lady." He got up and paced back and forth, never going more than six feet in either direction. "You've got some news, I can tell. Don't hold out on me. I've waited too long. She promised she would get back here two weeks ago and I've been going nuts!"

He stopped and stared at me intently. I could see him trying to get a handle on his emotions. Then he smiled—an unbelievably sweet and charming smile.

"You've got to understand what it's like in here. A guy like me...I don't belong. You can see that, can't you? Beth could. That's why she wants to help me. That's why she promised to hire one of those fancy criminal lawyers from Atlanta—one of the 'ponytails'—a smart guy who can get me out of here."

He sat back down and leaned in closer to whisper, "We're going to get married, me and Beth, and go live in France where she can write novels and I can...well, she says I can fulfill my destiny there."

"My, that is a grand idea," I observed, careful to hide my astonishment with this new turn of events. "I never realized you two had planned such an ambitious future together. How are you going to finance this venture? Has Beth sold her book?"

Jake Bradley sprawled back in the chair and chewed nervously on his bottom lip for a moment while he stared suspiciously at me. "I thought Beth sent you."

"Beth Davis is the reason I'm here," I admitted truthfully.

"What's going on, lady?"

I took a deep breath and begged Leonard not to desert me.

"Jake, your friend Beth has disappeared. I'm trying to find her."

I watched, fascinated as the blood drained from his face until his pale, finely chiseled features and sensuous lips reminded me of a beautiful marble statue by Donatello I had seen

135

once in a museum in Europe.

"Why aren't the police looking for her?" he asked in a quiet voice.

"They don't know the things I know."

The room was so silent I was afraid he could hear the pounding of my heart. I resisted the urge to wipe the moisture from my upper lip while I waited for him to speak. When he finally did, he surprised me.

"You got any cash?"

"Wha...what?"

"Money, moola, bills. Give me something—a fifty at least."

He was so intent—so persuasive—I don't hesitate for a moment. I reached around for my bag, took out my wallet and handed him two twenties and a ten. He took the money over to the one-way glass and tapped on it.

"Roy?" he called out. "Roy, I need to go to the can."

The door opened and Jake slipped the money to the guard on the other side. He sauntered back to the table with a grin on his face.

"Beth and I worked that out. For the right price, Roy turns off the microphone and looks the other way. You can trust him. He knows better than to cross me." The grin disappeared. A muscle twitched in its place. "Everybody knows better than to cross me. You hear that, Cousin?"

I ignored the threat. Jake Bradley might look like a sexy, smoldering volcano of a man, but I suspected that he was all smoke and mirrors. Nevertheless, it was easy to see why Beth Davis had fallen for him. He must have fit right in with her daydreams—and nighttime fantasies. I'm sure he turned on the charm and upped the wattage of that incandescent smile whenever she walked in the room. Poor little thing, I thought, she didn't stand a chance against a cheesy predator like him.

"Okay, lady. Now tell me just what you think you know about Beth."

My mind had been going a mile a minute, trying to piece together the bits of information he had dropped. I took a fairly educated guess.

"Beth was getting the money for your lawyer and your little European excursion from her blackmail scheme." I stopped.

His expression didn't change one iota, but I was sure I hadn't told him anything he didn't already know. I decided give him a little push. "Weren't you afraid for her? Those were rich and powerful men. They could have...."

Jake laughed derisively. "What? Canceled her ticket to the country club dance? Given her the wrong stock tip? Give me a break, lady. Those guys were nothing but wealthy losers—fat cats with too much inherited money and not a brain in their heads. Do you think we're stupid or something? We did some research with our own private Mr. Wizard. We made damn sure of our targets before we lifted a finger."

"Where did you get the idea in the first place?"

He looked at me intently. "Why should I tell you all this?"

"Because without Beth, your plans are in the trash bin, and since you're stuck in here, I'm the only one you can count on to find her."

"What's in it for you?"

"I have my own little agenda," I admitted. "But that's none of your business."

He glowered menacingly at me, but I had gotten over Jake Bradley. He didn't scare me anymore. I told him so. He laughed.

"You want to know about me and Beth. Okay, I'll tell you. A couple of years ago she got permission from the warden to interview a prisoner. He asked for volunteers. It's always good to volunteer. You get perks, if you know what I mean?"

I nodded. I had seen enough cellblock blockbusters. I knew what a pack of cigarettes or an extra hour in the exercise yard meant to a prisoner.

"Anyway, she liked me right off," his smile was smug and self-assured. "She asked if she could come back and talk to me again. It went on from there," he shrugged as though it were a foregone conclusion that every woman, given half a chance, would fall in love with him.

"After a while she wanted to get married. I told her it wouldn't work with me in here and her out there. I'd be jealous all the time." His smile was lazy and mocking. "I told her she had to get me out of here—get me a new lawyer. I was innocent—framed for something my ex-wife did."

"Were you?" I interrupted.

"What do you think?"

"I think you're very persuasive."

He smiled that wonderfully deceptive smile. "I like you, cousin," he whispered. "I like you a lot."

Underneath the designer aftershave that was probably a gift from Beth Davis, Jacob Bradley wore the sour smell of dirty underwear and sweaty sheets. There was a crust of dirt under the nails of his manacled hands and his fingers were stained yellow from cheap tobacco. I shrugged off a feeling of repugnance, and the desire to get up and run like a bunny for home. I still had work to do.

"I like you, too, Jake," I murmured shyly, the lie rolling easily off my tongue. "I can see why Beth fell so hard for you. Can't you think of something, anything, that might help us find her?"

He opened his mouth to speak but was interrupted by a knock on the door.

"Uh, oh."

"What's that?" I asked.

"Time to feed the monkey. Give me some more dough."

"I don't think I have much...."

"Sure you do," he said. "A fancy lady like you—with expensive clothes and a pricey watch."

I had left my bag on the table next to me. I reached for it but Jake grabbed it first. He held it between his knees and went through it roughly with both hands.

"Jake! Give it back," I ordered.

"Or what? You'll scream for help? If you do, that's the last you'll see of me," he warned.

"Well, well, look what we have here." Jake held up my key chain—the one with the small container of pepper spray on the end. "How come they let you in here with this?" he marveled.

"Roy was...."

"Roy is a smuck!" laughed Jake. "I'd better turn this over to him or you'll both be in a world of trouble."

"Why bother? They're not going to search me on the way out."

"Look, lady," he said gruffly, "I know what I'm doing."

Jake crossed the room and tapped on the door. When it

opened, he smiled and whispered something to Roy—then sprayed him full in the face with the pepper spray. Before the guard could scream, Jake grabbed him by the throat and dragged him into the room. I sat glued to my seat with horror as he slammed the man's head into the wall again and again until he was unconscious. Roy slid to the floor and lay there, not moving even when Jake kicked the mountain of belly in disgust.

"Fat pig!" he spat. "Fat tub of guts!" Jake reached down and unholstered Roy's gun and stuck it in the waistband of his own jeans. He searched through the guard's pockets until he found the key to his handcuffs, and sighed with deep satisfaction as he released himself from their constraint.

He turned back to me and grinned. "Easy as pie! Thanks, Cousin Paisley."

"What the hell have you done?" I gasped, when I finally found my voice.

"Taken control of my future, little lady. I'm going to fulfill my destiny." His laughter was full of irony.

"What about Beth? Don't you care what happens to her?"

"The world is full of Beths—poor, sad, lonely little women dreaming of a guy like me. Pitiful little bitch. She's crazy for me, you know. Trouble is she's crazy, period. I deserve better than that."

He shook his head sadly. "I was afraid she wasn't going to be able to pull this off. It was too complicated: too many details. The best plans are clean and simple. I should have waited for somebody with a little more smarts. Somebody like you, Cousin." He grinned.

"But, hey! Now's our chance! It's just you and me, kid. How are we going to get me out of here?"

I swallowed back the hot, sour, taste at the back of my throat and fought the nausea that threatened. I had seen worse violence before, but this had been so unexpected. I had vastly underestimated Jacob Bradley. I blamed myself, but not too much. After all, he was in the business of conning people. That's what he had done all of his life. That was why he was here in this prison.

CHAPTER TWENTY-THREE

Jake Bradley hooked a long leg over the chair back and rested an elbow on his knee. He didn't have to point the gun at me. He and I both knew he could easily kill me before I made it to the door. And screaming for help would be useless—Roy was unconscious, or dead, and the microphone was turned off.

I was scared, but comforted by the thought that it was two against one: me and Leonard against Jake. Leonard was a master at getting out of tighter spots than this. I was counting on him.

"I'm waiting, Cousin," Jake reminded me. "Waiting for you to come up with an escape plan."

"I don't...."

"Now, now, let's get rid of that negative attitude. How did you get here?" he prompted. "You got a car outside?"

Oh, God! I prayed, please don't let this monster near Cassie.

"N...no!" I stammered. "A...a friend dropped me off. She, er, he's not due back for another hour or two."

Jake came around to my side of the table and leaned back against the edge. He caressed my cheek with his rough, dirty fingers. When I flinched, he shook his head in warning. "Be still, pretty lady. It's been a long time. I want to enjoy myself."

"Jake, you don't really want to do this," I pleaded.

He slapped me lightly with his open palm and ran his fingers around my face and over my lips.

"So soft," he sighed regretfully. "Too bad we'll have to put off our fun until later, Cousin, dear. Sooner or later, somebody's bound to come check on poor old Roy when he doesn't answer the intercom."

Jake jumped up and pounded the table with excitement.

"That's it!" He shouted. "The intercom!"

He grabbed me by the arm and propelled me out of the chair and across the room. When I stumbled over Roy's foot Jake kicked it angrily out of the way and pulled me into the hallway and into an observation booth. Jake pushed me inside and followed, locking the door behind us.

"Well, what do you know," he laughed, looking out of the one-way glass into the room we had just vacated. "How nice to be the shoe on the other foot."

I sat down in the corner and watched as he examined our surroundings. A small television monitor above the desk was aimed at the other door in the hallway. A control panel underneath offered four other views. Jake switched back and forth between them, grinning all the while.

"Damn, this is even better than I imagined," he laughed. "What did I say, Cousin, about the best laid plans—pure and simple. We can sit here snug as bugs in a rug and wait until they meet our demands."

"And just what are they, Jake? What do you think you're going to get out of this?"

"That's just it, Cousin! I'm going to *get out*! And you are going to help me."

Jake outlined his escape plan, improvising here and there as I pointed out the obvious flaws. I knew that helping him might be construed as aiding and abetting a criminal, but what the hell! I was trying to save my own hide. If I were going to be his hostage—the human shield he used to make his escape—I wanted the plan to work. I only hoped that once we were safely outside I could make my own getaway.

"You get on the intercom. See this button here," he pointed. "Tell the guard at the main desk who you are. Tell him that I've taken you and Roy hostage. Make sure he knows I have a gun and I'm not afraid to use it on you."

"Thanks a bunch, Jake. That just made my day."

"Don't worry, Cousin. You're my ticket out of here. And besides, nothing's going to happen to either one of us." He pointed again at the intercom button. "Now get on the horn."

The guard at the main desk answered immediately. He listened intently as I told him what had happened and read the list of Jake's demands.

"The money has to be in unmarked bills," I added, "nothing bigger than twenties. Put the suitcase with the clothes and the money in the trunk of the car. Leave the trunk open until we get there so he can see that everything is okay. No one is to come near the car at any time. If these instructions are not followed to the letter, he will kill me."

"Are you okay now, Miss?"

"I'm fine," I assured him. "Everyone will be fine as long as you do as he says."

"I'll have to talk to some people—the governor, for one—to arrange all this. You understand it might be awhile before I get back to you?"

Jake grabbed the intercom out of my hands and shouted into it. "You got two hours, O'Neil. You understand that?" And he slammed down the receiver. "I think that went very well, don't you, Cousin?"

I fell asleep. People were astounded later, when I told the story. No one would believe that I could relax under those conditions. They thought I was bragging. But they didn't understand. It wasn't courage. It was stress, and my body's way of preparing for what was to come.

I dreamt of Meadowdale Farm, as I often did when I was forced to be away from home. The dream was very real. I could hear Cassie's Gypsy Kings CD playing softly on the back porch, and see the dragonflies dance over the patio as the tiles gave up their heat to the deepening twilight. There was a muted conversation in the background—a murmur of endearments and contented laughter. It was so beautiful I wept.

I woke up abruptly. Jake was shouting.

"I said, no, dammit!" He slammed his fists on the desk to make his point. "Fifty thousand dollars—no more, no less. And I don't give a shit how late it is. Tell that fat-assed banker this little lady's blood will be on his hands if he doesn't come through with the money. And, O'Neil," he added in a dangerously quiet voice, "you've got forty minutes."

Jake was furious. While I had slept, the charming con man had disappeared and something evil had taken his place. I could smell his fear—a fear that could make him even more dangerous. I grimly lowered my odds of getting out of this alive.

Jake paced up and down the narrow room, kicking my

chair viciously each time until I wised up and moved even further back in the corner. Once he stopped in front of the door and slammed his fists against it, screaming obscenities until he was hoarse.

O'Neil came back on the intercom less than two minutes before the deadline.

"Jacob? Are you there?" he asked in a carefully controlled voice.

"Yes, I'm here, you shithead! Did you get everything I wanted?"

"Yes, Jake."

"Fifty thousand...?"

"Fifty thousand dollars in small bills and two changes of men's clothing—size 32 waist—shoes size 10. All in a soft-sided zippered suitcase in the trunk of a black 1998 Chevy Camero with no plates—just like you ordered."

"And the television cameras?"

"Out front. All three national channels are represented by the local stations in Weiuca City, and CNN even sent a crew to cover the breaking news."

"And they've already broadcast the story at least twice over the local radio and television stations?"

"Some of them have stayed on with coverage since the story broke, Jake. Everybody is anxious to see you get blown away in living color."

"Shut up, you bastard! Shut up!" Jake grabbed me and pulled me over to the intercom. He shoved the receiver in my face and slapped me viciously. I cried out against my will. The blow was painful, but the surprise of the attack was what undid me.

"You hear that, O'Neil?" screamed Jake. "That's who's going to get blown away—and maybe a whole lot worse if you screw with me."

He slammed down the intercom and sagged against the desk with his head in his hands. At that moment, when I saw the terrified little boy who had gotten into a situation that was way over his head, I almost felt sorry for him.

"Give it up, Jake," I said softly. "This is a game you can't win."

"I've got no choice, Cousin," he insisted, his voice husky

with stress. I have to go through with this. And that means you do, too. Better get ready. We'll be taking off in a minute."

I listened desperately for Leonard's voice. Where was the wisecracking, sharp-minded detective when I needed him? All I could think of was a foolish rhyme I had learned as a little girl: "When in danger—when in doubt—run in circles—scream and shout!"

Jake watched the big wall clock above the desk. At six o'clock on the dot he pulled the gun out and pointed it at my head. His hand was steady and his voice calm. He appeared to have conquered his demons.

"We're going to do this, Cousin. Just you and me," he chuckled, "and baby makes three."

Jake opened the door carefully and pushed me outside with the muzzle of Roy's gun resting against my left earlobe.

"See anybody?" he whispered.

I shook my head. I couldn't believe it. The ugly hallway was as empty as when I had first seen it. Where was Superman when you needed him?

Jake stepped out in back of me and pulled my body close to his—the gun still against my head.

"My, but you do feel good, Cousin," he murmured, his breath hot and moist against my other ear. "Maybe I'd better revise my plans."

"Wha...what plans? What are you really going to do with me, Jake?"

He pushed me hard in the small of the back and jabbed the gun painfully against my temple. "Shut up!" he snapped. "You'll find out when it's time. Now move!"

I bade a prayerful farewell to everyone I had ever loved as we made our way slowly down the hallway to the big front doors of the prison. I had plenty of time and nothing else to distract me. It was a long hallway and we did not pass a single, solitary soul. The guards had obeyed Jake's orders to the letter and stayed completely out of sight.

Jake made me open the door and peek outside. I saw nothing but blinding white lights.

"Tell them to turn down the lights. Now!"

The crowd of was hushed and quiet—somber, as though waiting for an execution. When the lights dimmed I squeezed through a crack in the doors with Jake stuck to me like a barnacle.

"Easy does it," he said. "Don't go down the stairs, yet." He turned to the reporters, "Got your cameras on, fellows?" he shouted. "I got something to say."

"Go ahead, Jake," called out one. "We've been live for two hours. We're ready anytime you are."

Another female reporter spoke quickly and earnestly into the camera before she also turned and signaled that she was set. "Go, Jake," screamed her overwrought producer.

"I got a message," Jake shouted into the three microphones held out towards him. "A message for my Baby," he ignored the curious murmur in the crowd and continued. "I love you, Baby! I need you! Meet me at your favorite spot as soon as you can! Okay?" He nodded curtly at the reporters, "That's all folks," he snarled. "Get those damn things out of my face!"

The crowd was no longer hushed. Reporters and newsmen turned and spoke rapidly into cameras or microphones, filling the audience in on their interpretations of Jake's cryptic message.

"What's going on, Jake?" I whispered urgently.

"Jealous, honey?"

"Don't be stupid! Have you changed any of the plans we made without telling me?"

"You'll know soon enough. Meanwhile, I'll give you a clue: we're not going anywhere in that stupid redneck car."

"What the hell?" I gasped. "Why not? How else are you planning to get out of here?"

"Answer to the first question," he sneered. "That fancy little vehicle probably has at least five transmitters hidden inside. The cops would know every move I made. They could take their own sweet time setting up roadblocks and grab me whenever they felt like it. The suitcase is probably hot, too—and the shoes. The clothes are probably okay," he added thoughtfully. "Be hard to hide one of those gizmos inside a pair of pants or a tee shirt."

"Okay!" I hissed impatiently. "So what are you going to do? Swim your way out of here?"

He laughed softly in my ear. "Bingo!" he whispered.

CHAPTER TWENTY-FOUR

I struggled against Jake's grip, trying desperately to squirm out of his arms. His words terrified me more than anything else that had happened. Running for my life in a souped-up hillbilly mobile with a crazy-as-a-loon sociopathic killer seemed like a picnic in the park compared to sticking my big toe in that rampaging river.

"No!" I cried. "No, please!"

Lights flashed as cameras turned their attention back to me. If Gran or Cassie were watching the newscast, they would hardly recognize the pale and anguished face of the terror-stricken woman on the prison steps. With my wild and tangled hair, my wrinkled and disheveled clothes—I looked like a red-headed Irish banshee in the monitors I glimpsed as I passed by the camera crews.

Jake held me tightly against his body—the gun bruising my temple.

"Hold still, bitch! You got no choice. You either die right now on these steps with a bullet through your brain, or you help me and maybe you live. Which is it?"

He gave my ribs a painful squeeze, robbing me of breath and a voice. All I could do was nod.

"Okay! That's more like it. Now, listen up. We're going to make our way slowly to the car—just like we're really planning to leave that way. We take the money out of the trunk like we're counting it, only we stuff it in our pockets instead. You get a shirt and a pair of pants out of the suitcase and tie them around your waist. It'll be something for me to hold on to when we're in the water."

"Jake, no! You're...that's crazy," I whispered hopelessly. "We can't possibly survive out there...and in the dark?"

His answer was another shove as we started slowly down the long flight of steps. We moved awkwardly, like conjoined twins—each with a different destination in mind.

I searched the crowd for Cassie but didn't see her sweet face anywhere. And the only car in the riverfront lot where I had left her was the Camero. I was glad Cassie wasn't there. I didn't want her to see how scared I was. But most of all, I didn't want her to see me die.

Like the Red Sea, the crowd parted in front of us as we made our way slowly through the tangle of reporters and television cameras. Jake never let up his cruel hold on me. My breath was coming in ragged gasps, and I knew if I lived until tomorrow my ribs would be covered with bruises.

When we got to the car, Jake motioned for everyone to stay well away from us. He pulled me around to the back and looked inside the trunk.

"This is it, Cousin! Fifty thousand big ones—not too much and not too little. Just enough so they won't go crazy trying to find it, and yet enough for a new start. And best of all, they didn't have time to get sequential numbers. We'll be home free!"

"Then why not use the car?" I begged. "We can get a few miles away and ditch the damn thing in the woods. We can hitch a ride—be miles away before they find it. Please, Jake!"

"Shut up! I've made up my mind! They only way to win is to play by my own rules. The car is their game piece. I got my own way out of here. Now, take off your jacket and stuff these bills in your pockets. Pull on this tee shirt and tie the pants around your waist."

"But how can I swim...?"

"There's no swimming in that river," he hissed. "The current will take us where we want to go. Think of the money in your pockets as insurance that I won't let you drown."

Jake released his hold on me for the first time. I sagged against the car for a moment to catch my breath. The night was cool and clear, the air fresh and sweet. I breathed deeply, thinking that each breath might be the last before my lungs filled with the dirty brown waters of the Cumberland River.

"Move it!" ordered Jake. "We haven't got all night. I want to be in the water and away from here before they get the helicopter up in the air."

"Helicopter?" I asked hopefully. Helicopters, I knew, could hover over the water and rescue drowning swimmers.

"Yes, stupid! This isn't the first time somebody has tried to break out of this hellhole. I know the drill. When they close off the road, they swoop down out of the blue with a big searchlight and that's all she wrote. Lots of guys have tried to get out of here, but I'm the first one who going to make it!"

"And don't get any ideas about being rescued, Cousin," he sneered as he correctly guessed my thoughts. "With any luck at all, we'll be long gone before they get that whirly-bird in the air."

Jake took the money out of the suitcase and divided it between us. I stuffed as much as I could in my pant's pockets and put the rest inside my blouse before I pulled on the tee shirt and tied the pant's legs around my waist. Jake tugged on the knot and grinned.

"Good job, Cousin! Now listen up. We're going to walk around this side of the car like I'm a real gentleman who's helping you get in. When I open the car door, that's the signal."

Tears slid unbidden down my cheeks. Leonard had deserted me. There was nothing left but a frightened woman—a mother and a daughter who wanted nothing more than to tell her own mother and daughter how much she loved them.

"Signal for...?"

Jake grabbed my upper arms and held me in a cruel embrace.

"Don't you screw this up, bitch!" he snarled. "When I say 'jump,' you jump! Got that?"

I was numb—resigned. The truth was there was no other choice, and I thought, who knows but what the crazy son-of-bitch was right. Maybe we could get out of this alive. And then I remembered the river as Cassie and I had seen it that afternoon—the rolling, boiling waters that raced swiftly past—holding that frail little tree in its deadly embrace—and I knew there was only a very slim chance of us lasting even a few seconds.

As I followed Jake around the car, I formulated a tiny plan—something that just might work if the timing was right. When he gave the signal, I could turn and run toward the river with him, but instead of jumping, I would fall back and let him jump in and be swept away. Then I would be free—the nightmare would be over. I clung to that thought as he opened the car door and bent down, pulling me with him.

"Ready, Cuz?" he asked, his voice trembling with nervous excitement.

"Yes."

"Then, GO!" he shouted and pulled me with him toward the river. We ran across the ten feet of gravel that separated the parking lot from the river's bank—a thin, narrow strip of red mud that sucked at our shoes and slowed us down.

"Hurry!" Jake screamed. "Hurry!"

He almost pulled my right arm out of its socket as I struggled to pull my shoes out of the mire.

"Lose the shoes, stupid!" he shouted. "I can hear the helicopter!"

I pulled my bare feet out of the mud and we raced side by side to the river. When we got to the edge I pulled back with all of my strength, trying desperately to escape his grasp, but he was too strong. He grabbed my waist, wrapped his arms tightly in the pant's legs I had tied around me and threw us headfirst into the dirty waters of the Cumberland.

I don't remember much about that time in the water except in my nightmares—the ones that wake me with a pounding heart and sweaty sheets. I do recall, however the massive, bone-chilling cold, the taste of dirt and grit in my mouth, and the feeling of utter helplessness in the grip of a mighty power.

We twisted and turned, sometimes under the water, sometimes on top. Once I saw two moons, and I realized one must be the helicopter searching for us in the dark. I called out—screamed for help and got a mouthful of water instead. I choked and coughed, and went under again. It was quiet underneath the waves—another world—a world of silence and darkness where I was dying.

At some point I must have passed out because I woke up in the shallows, my knees scraping painfully against the rocky bottom. Jake struggled to his feet and pulled me to the shore where I lay gasping like a beached whale.

"I...we, we made it," I whispered. "I can't believe it. We're alive."

Jake laughed, a triumphant shout of exhilaration. "Damn right, we're alive!" he whooped. He coughed and spat dirty water on the beach. "But we can't stay here. They'll start searching the shore after a while—for our dead bodies," he snickered. "Fools!"

"Where are we going?" I looked around in the dark and saw nothing but the vast stretch of water in front of us. "Where is there to go?"

"Up there," he said pointing in the darkness.

I followed his finger with my eyes, my head falling back on my wet shoulders as I looked up at the sheer cliff behind us.

"Oh, no!" I gasped.

"Oh, yes!" he laughed. "We're almost home, Cousin. And we have to hurry. Baby's waiting."

"But that...there's no place to put your feet or hands."

"Around the other side," he explained impatiently. "We can climb over those boulders and grab onto the scrub growing out of the base. There's plenty of handholds. Baby told me."

"Who the hell is this baby you keep talking about?" I asked impatiently. "Are you just making this 'baby told me' stuff up so I'll do what you say?"

Jake laughed and pulled me to my feet. His eyes glittered in the dark like a cat's.

"I always gave you a choice, Cuz."

"Yeah," I agreed sarcastically. "Your way, or the highway."

"Or worse," he said pulling the gun out of his shirt.

"Will that thing fire after it's been in the river?" I asked skeptically.

"You don't really want to find out, do you?"

I stumbled after Jake as he climbed over the boulders to the base of the bluff that rose some twenty feet above us. My clothes hung wet and heavy against my cold and clammy skin and made walking difficult. I longed to tear away the extra layers but I was afraid to stop—afraid that Jake would decide he didn't really need me any more.

He pulled me up on top of the last big boulder and pointed to the vines and scrub that grew out of the side of the rocky cliff.

"You can hold on there," he said, squinting against the

dark. "And there, and then further up you'll see where to go. I'll be right behind you. And so will this." He patted the gun in his pocket and grinned. "Now let's go meet Baby."

CHAPTER TWENTY-FIVE

I fought my way slowly up the rocky face of the bluff inch by inch, clinging like a tree frog with all the strength in my fingers and toes. Once I even held onto a small branch with my teeth while I tried to get find a handhold in the friable sandstone.

My shoulders ached, my legs trembled with fatigue, and my hair and face were covered with dirt from the scree that showered back on my head as I crawled up the cliff.

Each time I paused to get my breath I said a little prayer— a petition for the strength to hang on for just another inch or two, and then another and another. I was almost at the top when I gave out completely. No matter how hard I tried I could not move another muscle. I clung to side of the cliff, afraid to breathe—afraid the slightest movement would cause me to slip and fall to the rocks below.

"Move, it on up!" shouted Jake from somewhere beneath me. "I said, move it, bitch!" he shouted again, giving me a shove.

My right foot slipped as the dirt crumbled beneath my toes. I dug my hands and fingers into the sandstone and held on for dear life to my precarious hold.

"No, please," I whimpered. "I...I can't."

Jake response was loud, angry and obscene. He reached up and found purchase over and above me. For a few dreadful moments I was afraid he had abandoned me to what would surely be my death. I was losing hope when I felt his hand close over mine.

"Come on, Cousin," he said, gritting his teeth with the effort. "Help me out here. I won't let you fall, but you've got to keep moving."

Somehow I managed to climb the rest of the way to the low stone wall at the top of the cliff where Jake was braced as he hauled me up. I fell over the wall and lay gasping and panting, tears of exhaustion and relief streaming down my face.

I looked around in the moonlight, astonished to see that I was in the clearing where Horatio and I had ended up after our wild ride around the lake. We were on top of the bluff overlooking the river and the prison.

I started to thank Jake for saving my life but he didn't give me a chance. He tore his pants and shirt from my body, and ripped my own clothes as he retrieved the money from my pockets and blouse.

"You're more trouble than you're worth, Cousin," he said, shaking his head. "I thought I would need you for the rest of the trip, but a worn-out, beat-up hostage is nothing but a drag. Sorry."

He took the gun out of his shirt and pointed it at my head. I didn't even have time to scream before he pulled the trigger.

"Damn! Damn! Damn!" he swore, as he tried over and over again to fire the waterlogged gun.

Terrified and shaken, I crawled away from him. He was too furious to even notice until I had almost reached the edge of the woods.

"Come back," he shouted. "There's more than one way to skin a cat. Even if this damn thing doesn't work." He turned and threw the gun as far as he could in the direction of the river.

"Thank you, boy," said a voice from somewhere on the other side of the clearing. "That's just the kind of stupid thing I was hoping a jackass like you would do."

"Who the hell is that?" yelled Jake. "That you, Baby? Daddy's going to be mad if you brought somebody with you."

"Jake, darling! You must forgive me," cried Bethlehem Davis as she rushed into the clearing. "I couldn't help it. I've lost everything—my house, my car—everything but the clothes I'm wearing. I had to have some help. It's all right, I swear, my darling. Oh, I've missed you so!"

Beth would have thrown herself into his arms if Jake hadn't held out his hand like a traffic cop and stopped her.

"Who the hell are you talking about?" he demanded.

Beth's face was white and anxious in the bright beam of a flashlight.

The man who held the light on her like a Broadway spot stepped out into the clearing. "Me," he laughed, "just little old me."

"And who the hell are you?" insisted Jake.

"It's Mike, Michael Davidson," explained Beth nervously. "You know, Mr. Wizard, the man from the newspaper who knows everything about everybody."

I pulled myself up and leaned back against a tree trying to gather my strength, hoping to make a break for it when I got a chance. The moonlight shone brightly on all the players on my little stage. I watched intently, fascinated, as they acted out their drama.

Beth turned back and forth between Mike and her lover, her orange skirt—the same one she had worn to my interview—swirling like a cheerleader's uniform with her movements.

"Mike's going to help us, Jake," she explained. "He's got a car, and some dry clothes, and...."

"And a gun," Mike interrupted with a snicker. "So if you don't mind, Jacob, sit down on that wall and put your hands up!"

Beth whirled on Mike, for once her words short and to the point.

"What are you doing, you horrid little man? You promised to help me!"

"And you promised to bring home the bacon, missy! You're the one who screwed everything up. I had the perfect plan! All those idiots with skeletons in their closets that only I knew about—and those beautiful video tapes! We could have cleaned up if you hadn't wasted all that time romancing this rotten little felon!"

"But I love Jake!" shouted Beth. "And he's innocent! A better lawyer...."

"Any lawyer worth his salt would soon find out the same thing everybody in Rowan Springs knows but you—that Jacob Bradley got drunk and killed a man in a barroom brawl."

Beth turned back to Jake, her face streaked with tears.

"But you told me it was your wife's fault, right, Jake? She

was flirting with that man—coming on to him. You were just defending your family's honor."

"Yeah, like Jacob Bradley gives a damn about family honor! He stole money from his old man the whole time he was growing up, and he sent his mother to an early grave. The only useful thing he ever did in his whole life was to give you a reason to help me with my blackmail scheme. I deserved that money," Mike whined. "Those rich wastrels looked down on me all their lives. To them I was nothing but the ink-stained little man who helped print the society page of the newspaper—the page that showed them enjoying the kind of life I've always wanted. And I could have had it all! With the kind of money they were coughing up I could have left this miserable little town and lived the rest of my days in comfort."

"But what about me and Jake?" cried Beth.

"As soon as I get my hands on the money, you are going to join my dear little wife Gladys in the eternal celestial dirt nap. And as for Jacob, well, who would believe a thief and a murderer?"

"You beast!" screamed Beth as she launched herself at Mike like an orange torpedo.

Mike raised the gun slowly and deliberately, aiming over her head. One second after he pulled the trigger Jake slipped to the ground with a look of utter disbelief on his handsome face, his hands covering the dark red stain on his wet tee shirt. Mike grinned as the younger man fell to his knees, grunting in pain.

"So much for true romance," he laughed.

Beth's heartbroken screams ripped through the night. She turned back to Jake, still screaming as she ran to his side. In her haste, she tripped—an ungainly step, as unexpectedly awkward as a stumbling gymnast whose beauty and grace is stolen by the sudden encounter with a splinter on a balance beam or a wrinkle in the floor mat. She hit the low stone wall with enough momentum to force the air out of her body. That grunt turned into a startled cry as she realized she was going over the cliff. There was a bright flutter of orange—the flicker of a dying flame—as she fell end over end to the dark waters below.

"Well, well, well," said Mike with a wondering tone in his voice. "The gods must indeed be crazy. I really didn't expect that little bit of good fortune."

He approached Jake's body with caution, circled him once, and kicked him in the stomach to make sure he posed no further danger before he bent down to retrieve the money.

I was numb with shock and exhaustion, but I knew I had to get away while his attention was elsewhere. I backed slowly out of the clearing and into the darkness of the surrounding forest.

The blinding light from his flashlight found my face and stopped me as surely as a bullet.

"Not so fast, lady," he ordered. "Now I guess you know why they say curiosity killed the cat. You should have kept your nose out of other people's business."

"Drop the gun, Davidson," commanded a familiar voice from the darkness.

"Who...who is that?" screeched Mike, as he flashed the light around the edge of the clearing. "Is this some kind of a joke?"

"I could say, 'the joke's on you,' but that is an unbelievably hackneyed phrase. I prefer to suggest that you are merely a greedy little scofflaw who is too careless and stupid to take even the most elemental of precautions. Or maybe it was arrogance that kept you from covering your tracks and thereby allowing me to follow you and your pitiful little protégée out here tonight."

"Horatio!"

"Be still, Paisley, dear. Don't come any closer, please. Mr. Davidson and I have some business to negotiate."

CHAPTER TWENTY-SIX

I strained my eyes trying to pierce the darkness, trying to discover where Horatio was hiding. One moment he seemed to be behind me, and the next he was ten feet away. Mike must have been just as confused. His voice went up an octave as he shouted out apprehensively, "Stop moving around! If you want to talk to me, dang it, then you'd better be still!"

"Of course, I want to talk to you, but you'll have to put the gun down before we can get serious," explained Horatio, from the other side of the clearing. "Guns make me nervous. Don't guns make you nervous, Michael?"

Mike's hand trembled as he held his weapon straight out from his body and turned in circles trying to aim in the direction of Horatio's ever changing position.

"Stop! Stop it!" he cried, rubbing his bald, sweaty forehead. "You're making me dizzy!"

"Oh, dear," offered Horatio politely, from a completely different spot, "I do apologize."

"Then, stop right now, or the little lady's going to pay for it."

I was the one who let Horatio down. I didn't see it coming. Mike lurched across the clearing and grabbed me before I knew what had happened. It was my startled cry that caused my dear friend to make his first mistake.

"Let her go," he said, stepping out of the protective cover of darkness. "Be a gentleman, and let the lady go."

Horatio looked lean and dangerous dressed in black. His white hair was covered by a black knit cap and his handsome face was smeared with camouflage grease paint. The tall, dignified, man about town who was my mother's bridge partner had once again become the intrepid cloak-and-dagger operative of his youth. He leaned casually against a tall pine and stuck his hands in his pockets.

I tried to turn, to pull myself away from Mike; but for the second time that night a gun barrel was shoved painfully against my ear and I was forced to endure the rough embrace of a desperate man.

"Let her go," repeated Horatio calmly. "She had nothing to do with this."

"The hell she didn't," spat Mike. "Bethlehem Davis was totally under my thumb until she met this bitch. Then she's all, 'oh, a real writer is going to read my manuscript'!" he mimicked cruelly. "Stupid little twit! I never realized she had written down all the dirt I told her about everybody in Rowan Springs until then. That's why I had to get it back. It was the blueprint for my future. I was going to make a million bucks between that and the videos we had of certain people's lunchtime quickies. That was all my idea, too," he boasted. "I had her set the stage—buy all that sexy underwear and stuff, and I brought in the big fish who couldn't refuse that kind of bait."

His laughter had a wicked edge, "Beth didn't want to operate the camera. Stupid girl said it wouldn't look good for her so-called writing career. I had to start filming at night and depend on those little audiocassettes. Made it harder to identify my, er, clients. Cut down on the profit."

I bit back a cry as he jabbed the gun into a tender spot on my temple.

"So, don't tell me this gal had nothing to do with making it all fall apart. And for that she deserves to die right here on the spot."

"Wait...," began Horatio.

"I didn't say I was going to do it," interrupted Mike. "I'm not an idiot. I know she's my ticket out of here—her and Jake's money. At least I got that," he muttered to himself. "So throw down your gun and starting climbing down that cliff to the river. Once you're down there I'll her go and make my escape.

"Don't go!" I cried involuntarily before Mike jabbed me in the stomach with his free hand.

"Don't worry, Paisley. I don't believe him," assured Horatio. "No, Michael, you must release Paisley before we negotiate any further."

"Then here!" screamed Mike. "Take her!"

He shoved me to the ground and fired three times at Horatio. I raised my head and saw my friend close his eyes and stiffen in pain.

"Horatio!" I sobbed, then watched unbelievingly as fire blossomed from his pocket and a neat little black hole appeared in the middle of Mike's bald pate. The man collapsed slowly, dying as he fell.

I scrambled hastily across the clearing on all fours to Horatio's side. I tried to brace him up against the tree, but his dead weight was too much for me.

"Anna," he whispered hoarsely. "Tell Anna...," and together we slid to the ground where my tears mingled in the dirt with his blood.

I cried all night, that night. I cried softly as I knelt by Horatio's side in the ambulance as it screamed through the darkness to Weiuca City and the Intensive Care Unit. And later I sobbed hysterically beneath the hot spray of the shower in the nurse's lounge as I cleaned up. I sobbed with complete abandon as though the tears would wash away the terrible memory of what had happened. And, against my will, I cried again when I called Mother to tell her where I was and the terrible thing that had happened.

By the time Mother and Cassie arrived it was almost dawn, and, thankfully, I was all cried out for their tears were just beginning.

They let Mother in to see Horatio just before they took him to surgery. Don't stay long the doctor said, I shouldn't waste any time but you may not have another chance to say goodbye.

Horatio was in surgery for hours. I finally persuaded Mother to get some rest after the surgeon came out at noon and said we couldn't see him until that evening—if he lived until then.

The hospital offered motel rooms across the street to visiting family members. My thoughtful daughter had gone ahead and found us a suite with two king-sized beds and a kitchenette. When we arrived, she had hot cocoa and sandwiches waiting.

I was still wearing the scrubs a considerate nurse had lent me after my shower. My own clothes were ruined—torn and covered with Horatio's blood. After hugging Cassie almost hard enough to break her sweet bones, I gratefully slipped into my own pajamas and robe that she had brought along with some clean underwear, shirts and jeans.

"My, this feels good," I said with a grateful sigh as I lay back on the pillows. "Oh, my." And the flood of tears started all over again.

Cassie and I fell asleep hand in hand on the big bed.

I don't know if Mother slept at all. When I woke up, stiff and sore and barely able to walk, around six o'clock in the evening, she was still sitting in the rocking chair by the window—her own bed as neat and tidy as she looked.

"Good evening, Mother," I whispered, anxious not to awaken Cassie. "Are you okay?"

"Yes, dear," she answered, her voice a soft monotone.

"Eaten anything?" I asked, as I hungrily eyed the unappetizing film over the cold cocoa and the hard crusts of the sandwich bread.

"No, dear."

I stuck my finger in the cocoa and swirled it around, removing the chocolate scum before I raised it to my lips and drank it down. Pretending the hard crusts of the pimento cheese sandwich was toasted bread, I ate one and had started on another when I heard a quiet sob.

"Muufther?" I asked with my mouth full.

"What have I done, Paisley?" she cried, her voice full of the deep searing pain in her soul. "Oh, dear, God! What have I done?"

Horatio's heart stopped twice during the early hours of the evening. Only his valiant spirit and the skill of his doctors brought him around, but the surgeon warned us that he might not have much time. We should make the most of it, he cautioned, because Horatio did not have the strength left for another rally.

Mother went in to see him first. Unable to tear my eyes away, I watched through a small slit in the blinds over the window to the ICU as she patted his sheets softly into place and smoothed the white hair back from his brow. Her touch was gentle and full of the love she had come so close—might still be close—to losing forever.

"Horatio," she whispered softly. "Horatio, my darling. You

must get well. We have a wedding to attend."

He opened his tired eyes slowly and, too weak to speak, questioned her with a look. "No, dear," she smiled. "Not Cassie, or Paisley, either. It's ours—our wedding, dearest Horatio."

The corner of his mouth turned up slightly in the sad parody of a smile before he lost consciousness again.

CHAPTER TWENTY-SEVEN

During the next two weeks, Horatio underwent two more operations. His doctors gave us little hope at first; but then, surprised by the miracle of his will to live, they fought as hard as he did to save his life.

Mother never left his side. When Cassie and I went home to Meadowdale Farm, she rented a small efficiency apartment near the hospital so that she could spend every waking hour with her patient.

Horatio was discharged from the hospital into a rehab center where, for two months, Mother worked diligently with the nurses and therapists to help him regain his former strength and agility. It was a hard, back breaking job and the nurses soon learned to love and respect the woman they all called "The Iron Maiden" as much as her patient did.

Cassie and Aggie and I missed them. The big old house seemed bleak and empty without their presence. We found things to do: I finished the last draft of Leonard's latest book, Cassie built a new web page for the coffee shop, and Aggie slept a lot, but we missed them.

In early November, almost three months after that terrible night, Mother called with the happy news.

"We're ready to come home, dear! Isn't that wonderful? I've convinced Horatio to occupy the summer suite, until the wedding that is."

I chuckled. I could almost see her blush.

"So, if you don't mind, maybe you and Cassie could get things...."

"We've already done it Mother. We've aired out, cleaned up, and put on fresh new everything. Apollo watched the baby last Monday, and Mabel spent all day with me and Cassie. We went to the grocery and bought all of Horatio's favorite things. And I made a wine run to Morgantown for that fancy Sherry he likes. Oh, and I even called Horatio's houseman and asked him to pack a couple of bags. I'll pick them up this afternoon. So, you can see, we're all set."

"You've missed us," she astutely observed.

"A bunch!"

The ride home exhausted Horatio. He sat in the library before a blazing fire for only thirty minutes before he begged our pardon and asked to be excused.

Cassie and I stayed when Mother told us they would be fine. She had gotten used to tucking her invalid into bed. We sat and stared at the fire, neither one wanting to be the first to admit how weak and frail our friend looked.

I broke the ice first. "Mother doesn't seem to notice," I added.

"I guess that means he looked much worse before," guessed Cassie.

"I'm afraid you're right, Toots. And I feel so guilty." I looked away, unable to stop the tears.

"You? Why on earth, Mom?"

"If it hadn't been for me...."

"Mom! Horatio was chomping at the bit, waiting for his moment to shine in Gran's eyes. When you were taken hostage that night, he called me."

"He did?"

"He told me to tell Gran not to worry. He was following a lead he knew would take him to you. He was going to save you to win her over."

"My, God! He didn't have to do that. She always loved him. It was her loyalty to Dad that kept her from marrying him."

"Well, something changed her mind."

"Apparently," I grinned, as I wiped away the tears. "And now we have a wedding to plan!"

Horatio gained strength daily. Mother was like a drill sergeant—relentless with his workout schedule. She had a Jacuzzi installed in a new greenhouse addition off her sitting room, and continued his exercises there—after his weight training every morning.

The Poisoned Pen, by E. Joan Sims

A week before Christmas, they announced that they were ready. The wedding was to be on December the twenty-seventh.

"But...but, Gran!" protested Cassie.

"Look, Mother," I admitted, "even a barbarian like me knows you can't get ready for a fancy wedding in less than a week."

"Who says I want a fancy wedding?" she laughed.

"Okay, forget the 'fancy,' but the invitations, the guests...."

"Paisley, dear, all the guests Horatio and I want are here already, except for dear Velvet and she's on safari and can't come anyway."

And so, with very little ado, we planned the not-so-fancy wedding of Anna Howard Sterling and Horatio St. Vincent Raleigh. The happy couple was married in the parlor of Meadowdale Farm at two o'clock in the afternoon, the Honorable Judge James Hershey presiding.

Cassie was her grandmother's maid of honor; and, in the absence of his nephew who was on his own honeymoon, Horatio graciously allowed me to stand up with him. Mother looked beautiful in a simple pale gray satin dress with matching Tahitian pearls—a wedding gift from the groom. I gave in and wore the black velvet pant suit and ruffled blouse she had given me for Christmas three years before, and Cassie—the only spot of color in our little wedding party—looked beautiful in a sapphire blue silk blouse and black satin skirt. When she walked in ahead of Mother, I had to choke back tears as I saw the diamond and sapphire cross her father had given her sparkling at her throat.

It was a beautiful wedding—short and sweet. Mother and Horatio had written their own vows. We all cried—even the judge. When it was over, Mother suggested that Horatio and Judge Hershey have a brandy in the library—Mother's way of insuring that Horatio would not overdo—and we scurried around making final preparations for the reception—my gift to the ceremony.

The table in the big dining room was laden with all of our favorite things: North Carolina brown-sugar-encrusted baked ham, mesquite smoked turkey, a platter of imported cheeses and exotic fruit, angel biscuits, country pate, quail eggs, marzipan, and three different kinds of potato salad. And on a small table in front of the windows sat a charming wedding cake—not too big and not too small—with "Anna and Horatio, Forever" written on the top.

When I insisted on giving the reception, Mother agreed only after I promised to invite just our closest friends. It was a wonderful, happy gathering of people who knew how close we had come to not being able to celebrate this day—how close we had come to having a darkness color all the rest of our days—so laughter, good cheer, and a wonderful gladness spread from one corner of the old house to the other as we poured sparkling wine and toasted the happy, and very lucky couple.

I tried to get Mother alone all afternoon. Something had been nagging at me ever since Cassie and I had talked about Mother's motives for giving in to Horatio's proposal. I didn't want to make her mad, but I was curious.

They had decided to spend their wedding night in a friend's cabin at the lake, with a longer honeymoon to come when Horatio was stronger. He had arranged for a limousine to pick them up at six, and when Mother went to her bedroom to finish packing I followed with an offer to help.

"Well, damn, Mother, looks like you've gone and done it!" I said, giving her a hug. "Congratulations."

"Paisley, darling, must you always be so...."

She smiled as she caught herself, too happy to chastise me on a day like this.

"Never mind, dear, and thank you for everything—especially for being the wonderful daughter that you are."

"Wow! You must really be happy."

She looked at me with the sweetest smile I had ever seen and winked. "You betcha!"

"By the way, Mother, I'm a little reluctant to bring up the subject, but I've just got to know."

"Hurry, dear. Horatio's waiting for me."

"Okay," I said, taking the plunge. "What have you decided about the...er, you know...."

"What, dear?" she asked impatiently.

"The graves," I blurted out. "Where you want to be buried and all."

"Oh, that."

She straightened her little velvet hat and adjusted the veil "just so" over the top of her elegantly curved eyebrows before she turned and gave me another wink.

"After a great deal of soul-searching, Paisley, dear, I've finally decided to leave that up to you."

ABOUT THE AUTHOR

E. JOAN SIMS was born in a delightful small town in Kentucky not unlike the fictitious "Rowan Springs" which is the home of Paisley Sterling, the heroine of her mystery novels.

After completing her graduate and postgraduate work at Emory University in Atlanta, Georgia, she became the Director of Medical Records at the newly built Holy Family Hospital, where she worked until she and her new husband left for a year in Barcelona, Spain. They returned to Georgia to pursue their careers, and then moved again—this time to Caracas, Venezuela, where they spent fourteen wonderful and exciting years.

When the family returned to the United States, Joan resumed her interesting work in disease surveillance at the Centers for Disease Control and Prevention, where she is still employed.

Writing is in her in blood. Joan's father published many short stories and poems in the popular magazines of the forties and fifties. Her dream was to place her own works next to his on the bookshelf in the family library. The publication of the Paisley Sterling Mystery series is the realization of that dream. Joan notes that there is plenty of room remaining on the bookshelf, and lots of mysteries waiting for Paisley to solve.

Be sure to visit her web site at:

www.ejoansims.com

Printed in the United States
81802LV00005B/118-138